THE TEARS OF THE  SALAMANDER

PETER
DICKINSON

THE TEARS OF THE SALAMANDER

WENDY
LAMB
BOOKS

Published by
Wendy Lamb Books
an imprint of
Random House Children's Books
a division of Random House, Inc.
New York

Visit us on the Web! www.randomhouse.com/kids
Educators and librarians, for a variety of teaching tools, visit us at
www.randomhouse.com/teachers

Library of Congress Cataloging-in-Publication Data
Dickinson, Peter.
  Tears of the salamander / Peter Dickinson.
    p.   cm.
Summary: When Alfredo, a twelve-year-old choir boy in eighteenth-century
Italy, loses his family in a fire, he goes to live with Uncle Giorgio, who he
discovers is a sorcerer in control of the fires of Mt. Etna with sinister
plans for his nephew.
  ISBN 0-385-73098-5 (hardcover) — ISBN 0-385-90125-9 (GLB) —
  ISBN 0-440-23823-4 (trade pb)
  [1. Magic — Fiction.   2. Fire — Fiction.   3. Salamanders — Fiction.
4. Singing — Fiction.   5. Uncles — Fiction.   6. Orphans — Fiction.   7. Etna,
Mount (Italy) — Fiction.   8. Italy — History — 18th century — Fiction.]   I. Title.
  PZ7.D562Te 2003
  [Fic] — dc21

                                                          2003000584

The text of this book is set in 11-point Stempel Garamond.

Book design by Trish Parcell Watts

Printed in the United States of America

February 2005

10 9 8 7 6 5 4 3 2 1

BVG

THE TEARS
OF THE
SALAMANDER

CHAPTER ONE

THE GIFT ARRIVED FOR ALFREDO'S SEVENTH name-day. It wasn't like his other gifts—the basket of candied cherries, the hobbyhorse, the toy drum—not a gift for a child at all. He opened the little leather pouch and pulled out a fine yellow chain, like the one his big brother, Giorgio, had been given to wear round his neck for his First Communion, but instead of a cross on the end this one had a funny little animal, made of the same yellow stuff as the chain.

He stared at it. The body was like that of one of the little brown lizards that lived in the cracks in the brickwork of the bakehouse, except that it had a long tail that curled under its belly, right round behind and over, with the end hanging down beside its front leg with a sharp hook at the tip. And the spread toes had small hooked claws, and not the sucker pads of the bakehouse lizards.

The head and face were even more different, not like any lizard's, but round and wrinkled, like the face of the little gray ape Alfredo had seen at the great Shrove Tuesday fair, sitting on a hurdy-gurdy with a leash round its neck.

Except that the monkey had had a huge wide grin, but this thing's mouth was a little round hole.

"That's a funny animal," he said. "What is it?"

Nobody answered. He looked up, puzzled, aware of an uncomfortable silence in the room.

"What is it, Mother?" he said again.

Mother sighed and looked questioningly at Father.

"It's a present from my brother, your uncle Giorgio," said Father. "To bring you luck."

"You're not going to let him wear it?" said Mother.

"Better than not letting him," said Father, in the voice he used to settle an argument.

"He came to my christening too," said Giorgio, "but he never came to my name-day, or gave *me* a present, and *I'm* named for him. He could've brought one when he came to Alfredo's christening, but he never even looked at me. I knew he was my rich uncle so I was set to charm the heart out of him, but he pushed straight past in his posh getup and kissed Mama's hand, all la-di-da. Then he hung over the cradle for a bit, and went off and stuffed himself at the sideboard like he hadn't eaten for a month."

"He didn't pay much attention to anyone," said Mother.

"Never does," said Father. "Better that way. And you are named for my grandfather, not your uncle."

There was an edge in both his parents' voices that Alfredo didn't notice but remembered later, looking back to what had happened on his name-day. At the time he was busy puzzling over the gift his uncle had sent him.

"Yes, but this animal," he said impatiently. "What is it?"

"It's a salamander," said Father, with a chuckle that

Alfredo, also later, realized must have been forced. "Perhaps it will bring you luck, little son of mine."

⚜

After the excitements of his name-day Alfredo found it hard to sleep. Restless, he crept down to the kitchen for a mug of water. There were cracks of light around the kitchen door, and the sound of Father's voice from beyond it. He hesitated. He caught a few words here and there.

". . . has no children, as far as I know . . . renounced my own birthright—I can't do that for him . . . make up his own mind when he is old enough to understand . . ."

Mother said something, too softly for Alfredo to catch, apart from the note of deep anxiety. Father sighed heavily and answered.

". . . must have its Master. That is the one thing on which he and I ever have been able to agree."

Alfredo crept back upstairs without his drink.

ℍ

But perhaps the salamander did bring Alfredo luck. Nobody had been able to tell him much about salamanders, except that they lived in the fire in the heart of certain mountains, and that if questioned they would tell you the truth. He was pleased by the bit about the fire. Though he lived in a hot country, he had always loved the bakehouse, especially the glorious moment when Father opened one of the fire-pit doors to add a fresh log, and the huge orange energy, a power like that of the sun, came streaming out. Oh, to live in the heart of such a fire, like a salamander!

3

So he wore his uncle's gift every day, hidden beneath his shirt, even for church, when Mother had asked him to take it off in case the priests found out. She was nervous of people, but especially priests, because Father distrusted and despised them and said so openly, and Mother was convinced the priests would learn about it and make the whole family do horrible penances. That was one reason why she was so bewildered when it was discovered that Alfredo had a singing voice.

There was no musicianship anywhere in the family. Father would bellow popular songs, all on one note, to the rhythm of his dough-kneading. Neighbors said it was hard to believe anyone could sing so badly if he wasn't doing it on purpose. And Mother would warble as she went about her work with a more varied but no more accurate use of the scale. When he was smaller, Alfredo's attempts to copy his parents had combined the worst of both styles, but now he seemed more to be singing for the sheer joy of doing so, unconsciously putting the tunes to rights as he went. Before long he was singing, or attempting to sing, everything he heard, from the indecent ditties of the sardine fishers to some part in one of the convoluted polyphonies of the cathedral.

Living near the center of the city, they went there to Mass. Shortly after they had emerged one Sunday, Alfredo was sitting on a low wall beside Mother, while Father argued guild business with a rival baker and Giorgio larked with some of his cronies across the square. As he waited Alfredo was trying to re-create something he had just been listening to, the *Nunc Dimittis* at the end of the service, with the high voice of a single choirboy floating like a gliding gull above the waves of sound from the rest of the choir, and then soaring on alone.

"*Lord, now lettest thou thy servant depart in peace,*" he sang, "*according to thy word. For mine eyes have seen . . .*"

A short, fat priest came stalking by, turned and stared at them. Mother gave her usual start of guilt.

"Don't stop, boy," snapped the priest. "Start at the beginning. . . . Louder . . ."

Astonished but delighted—nobody had ever bothered to listen to his singing before—Alfredo stood, filled his lungs and sang. The chatter around them stilled. People turned to listen. There were amused *bravos* as he allowed his voice to fade, as the choirboy's had done, into the noon stillness.

"The child has a voice," said the priest. "Who has been teaching him?"

"No one," stammered Mother. "I don't know where he got it from."

She made it sound as though Alfredo had picked up his talent in the street and was now being accused of having stolen it.

"Bring him to the cathedral, the small north door, tomorrow, a little before noon. Ask for me, Father Brava."

Father came striding across, his face stiff with anger.

"No!" he said. "Absolutely not! My son is a man, and must remain a man, and beget sons of his own!"

"The decision is not taken at this age," said the priest calmly. "The voice may not develop. The Prince-Cardinal is both humane and generous. He does not go against the wishes of the parents, but richly rewards those who consent. Meanwhile, your son will go to school, learn to read and write, both Latin and the common tongue. These are gifts not to be despised. You are a baker, I see from your dress. The patronage of the Prince-Cardinal is not to be despised, whereas his disfavor . . . But you are a sensible man, sir. I do not need to tell you that. Come too, with the boy, if your ovens can spare you, and you will be able to discuss matters with the Precentor. . . ."

Alfredo adored being a chorister. He made friends easily among the other boys, though they teased him for his southern accent, but he was more sober-minded than most of them and thus seldom in trouble. Several of them wore little charms and tokens around their necks, as well as their crucifixes, so he didn't need to take special trouble to hide his salamander, though he didn't go flashing it around. Even the schoolwork did not bore him. He was naturally neat and tidy, and soon wrote well and read Italian with fluency. Latin was harder, but he had the incentive of needing to know the meanings of the words he spent such long hours singing, because he felt in his heart that the meaning was part of the music, that even in the dispassionate, almost bloodless style of church music a word of grief must sound different from a word of rejoicing.

But it was the music itself that truly mattered. Those long hours were not long to him. The dullest choir practices, with endless repeatings and repeatings of a few short bars with which the choirmaster was dissatisfied, were time contentedly spent. This was what God had brought him

6

into the world to do. This was how he wanted to spend the rest of his life.

He understood now what Father had been talking about when he had objected so strongly to Alfredo's even being auditioned for the choir. Four of the adult choristers were castrati. That's to say they'd had their testicles removed when they were boys, in the same way that farmers gelded young male sheep and cattle so that they never became normal rams and bulls and could never sire young; it kept them docile and improved the flavor of their meat. But in the case of the choristers it meant that their voices had never broken, and they now sang alto or countertenor, instead of tenor or bass. They, too, could never become fathers.

The boys of course gossiped and joked about this, but as well as the castrati there were also four tenors and two basses in the choir, all of them once choirboys; some had taken only minor orders, and thus, not being true priests, had married and had children.

This possibility had done little to appease Father. If anything, he felt extra contempt for these half-priests, as he called them. His plan was that he would simply refuse to let Alfredo have the operation, and then hope that when the boy's voice broke, the resulting sound would cease to be pleasing to the ears of the Prince-Cardinal.

In fact, it was this prospect that Alfredo himself most dreaded. He would have preferred to end up as a tenor or bass, but rather than leave the cathedral altogether he would have chosen to undergo the pain and danger of the operation, and then the lifelong derision involved, and sing on. One of the countertenors, though elderly, still had the most marvelous voice. The Prince-Cardinal's favor had made him a rich man, but Alfredo could hear, plain in every note, that Brother Jesu-Maria sang for the pure joy of it.

He was lucky, of course, with his family living so close to the cathedral, that he wasn't entirely cut off from his old life. In midweek the Prince-Cardinal retired to his country estate for study and contemplation (in fact, as everybody knew perfectly well, to enjoy a nobleman's normal home life with a faithful wife, children—not all of whom were hers—and at least one mistress). Cathedral services were simplified and reduced so that the canons and other priests could do the same sort of thing, according to their resources and status, and after midday Mass the choirboys were left pretty well to their own devices, but with the certainty of savage beatings if they were late for evensong. Alfredo went home, singing as he trotted the few hundred yards through the steeply twisting narrow streets, almost empty now in the afternoon heat.

The day's baking would by then be finished. Mother and Father would be having their siesta. He would go through to the bakehouse, where Giorgio would greet him with "Late again, kid? Sure you can manage on your own? See you," before going off to join his friends and prowl, never with any success, for girls. Alfredo would then settle down to tend the ovens.

There were three of them, each with its own quirks and needs. Everybody, except for the other bakers, agreed that Father made the best bread in the city and for miles around, and ultimately his success depended on his skill in the management of his ovens, his ability to reach and maintain an exact, even heat, different for each oven, throughout the baking process. Any change of wind affected the draft in the flues, as did the temperature of the outside air; logs from different kinds of trees burnt hotter or cooler; bone-dry logs burnt too fast and hot to be useful, but too much moisture was worse than too little; and so on.

Father had built the ovens with his own hands, making them far more massive than those in any normal bakery, so that each, when thoroughly warmed through, would become a great block of heat around the hollow in which the pale dough magically turned itself into crisp and golden loaves. The ovens had first been lit long before Alfredo was born, and since then had never gone cold, but after each morning's baking was over they were allowed to rest for a while and then slowly, slowly reheated to be at the exact temperature needed for the next day's baking.

Each daily cycle began in midafternoon, with the ash being raked out of the fire pit and sifted into the barrow; the larger embers, still twinkling with sparks and veins of fire, were tossed back over the fire-pit floor; a layer of laths was spread above them, the door closed to a crack and the dampers opened, and the ashes were barrowed out to the tip and fresh logs barrowed in on the return journey from the drying stacks behind the house. By now the laths in the first oven were roaring, and dry logs, already in the bakehouse, could be inserted above them with the long tongs, the oven door closed, and its dampers half closed, and a start made on the second oven. By the time the third had reached this stage Alfredo would hear his parents' bed in the room above the bakehouse creak as his father heaved himself out, and a few minutes later that slow, distinctive tread would come down the stairs, and the door would open. Father would glance in each fire pit, open each oven and reach in to feel the heat, close it again and say something like "That's fine. Where's Giorgio? After the girls again? Fat chance. He shouldn't leave all the work to you."

"But I *like* doing it," Alfredo would say.

This was less than the truth. The feeling had grown only gradually since he'd left home, but by the time he'd been away for a year he had come to see that, in some way that he didn't understand, he would have missed looking after the ovens—by himself, without Giorgio—as much as he would have missed singing in the cathedral. Mysteriously it was the same kind of thing. He understood the ovens and their needs very much as he understood the music that he sang, the inwardness of it, its central nature. And not only the ovens. He could pick up a log from the stack and immediately sense the hidden heat within it, waiting to be woken by the flame, its intensity, its possible duration. He could sense the swirling climb of the drafts up the flues . . .

. . . and then, after the family meal—two hours earlier than usual, so that he could be back at the cathedral for evensong—he would go back to the bakehouse and stand in the middle of the floor and feel the glowing fire pits of the three ovens around him as a single larger fire, with himself in the midst of it, in the heart of the living flame—just as, in the middle of some pulsing *Gloria* in the cathedral, he was in the heart of the music. It was as though flame and music were only different ways in which a single, majestic power made itself manifest.

CHAPTER TWO

It was on such an evening, in Alfredo's twelfth year, that his whole world changed. He had left home a little early because he was singing one of the solos at evensong. With the Prince-Cardinal away the choirmaster was taking the chance to give the first-year seniors a turn so that when their time came to sing for the ears of His Eminence they would not be afraid. So Alfredo robed himself and settled into a corner of the vestry and bowed his head over his clasped hands in the attitude of prayer. He didn't understand about real praying. It was just words, the same words repeated and repeated until they were emptied of meaning. What he was really doing was allowing the fire of the bakehouse that still surged and swirled through his mind to turn itself gradually into the music that he was going to sing. He was more than happy. There were no words for it. Only the blessed souls in the presence of the Almighty could know and feel anything like what Alfredo knew and felt.

He heard a noise from the body of the cathedral. Not many people came to weekday evensong, often no more than a few old crones, but this was actual bustle, hurrying feet. A door must have been thrown open, because now there were sounds from outside, yells, clamor. More. Worse. The noises in themselves had nothing to do with Alfredo, with the fire and the music inside him. But these things too had changed. The music was gone. And the fire . . .

There was madness now in the fire, the wildness of wild beasts, the fury of a howling storm. He couldn't hold it. It would burst out of him, burn, kill . . .

He leapt to his feet. Several of his friends were just coming in through the vestry door, teasing each other—in whispers because the choirmaster was close behind them. Alfredo charged through, dodged the choirmaster's grab for him, ignored his bellow to stop, wheeled out into the chancel aisle, raced down through the screen and into the already darkening nave. Somebody had opened the great west doors, and through their arch he could see the orange glow of the blaze, the nearer roofs black against it, and above it the swirling tower of smoke, almost as black against the distant reds and golds and oranges of sunset.

He stood for a moment, panting, staring, then gathered up the skirts of his robes and pelted on down the twisting route along which he had so often trotted, singing. Long before he reached it, forcing his way through the gathering crowds, he already knew what he was going to find. His home, his ovens, were the roaring heart of that furnace.

A

They didn't punish him for missing evensong. He wouldn't have cared if they had—in fact he would barely have noticed. But the choirmaster, though strict, was a kindly man, and the boy's whole family had perished in the blaze. Besides, he had plans now for Alfredo.

"This is a terrible thing that has happened to you, my son," he said. "I truly grieve for you, as do all your friends here. You have no other relatives?"

"Only my uncle, Father. I don't know where he lives. He came to my christening, but I don't remember, of course. That's the only time I've seen him."

The choirmaster nodded. It didn't sound as if this uncaring relative would be much of a problem. Very likely he would be glad to have the boy taken off his hands.

"You need not sing if you do not feel up to it."

"Oh, sir, please," said Alfredo, weeping. "I *must* sing. It's the only thing left."

"That's a good boy," said the choirmaster, remembering minor turbulences in his own life during which he had taken refuge in music, and believing he understood something of what Alfredo felt. "Soon you shall sing a solo for His Eminence."

Next day an official from the City Watch came to talk to Alfredo. He did not, of course, explain that there was no doubt that the fire had started in the bakehouse, and that if it could be shown to be the baker's fault, then neighbors who had lost their houses as the flames spread would be able to claim against his estate, but if not the city would be liable for some kind of compensation.

Reluctant even to think about the fire, let alone talk about it, Alfredo admitted that he had been home that evening, had prepared the ovens for restarting their cycle, and had again been into the bakehouse after the family meal, shortly before he left, and everything had been normal. His parents had been upstairs in their room—he had heard voices there. (Bakers keep strange hours, and the early meal had interrupted their siesta.) Giorgio had gone out but he must have come back. . . .

"A young man was seen running into the house soon after the fire started," said the official. "Brave, but foolish, I'm afraid. I believe your father built his own ovens. He did not employ a professional? And he let you see to their firing, a child?"

Alfredo shook his head. How could he explain to this man that his father had known more about fire than anyone, and that there was no chance in the world that he could have made a mistake or not noticed if Alfredo had done so? Let alone how could he persuade him that there had been something wrong with the fire itself, its madness, its wildness, that it had somehow burst out of the fire pits like a wild beast bursting through the iron bars of its cage and going raging through the streets? And that Alfredo, sitting peacefully in the corner of the vestry, had felt the same thing happen to the hidden fire in his own heart, the fire that should have become music?

The choirmaster, sitting in on the interview, was not displeased. The boy, innocently admitting to the fact that he had been left alone to prepare the ovens, had provided the City with sufficient reason to declare the fire to have been the baker's fault, which made it even less likely that the missing uncle would appear to take the penniless orphan under his wing. It was already, thanks to the father's intransigence, a little late for the operation, but there had been certain scandals in the past, with expensive litigation to defend charges of kidnapping and mutilation. It was prudent, therefore that the consent of all interested parties—only the boy himself now, though an at least perfunctory attempt must be made to find the missing uncle—should be witnessed and registered in front of a notary.

Thus a fortnight later Alfredo found himself standing in front of the Precentor's desk. To the right of the desk, behind a folding table spread with documents, sat a fat little snuffling black-robed man whom Alfredo didn't know, but by his dress he was not a priest. Beyond him sat Father Brava. The choirmaster and another strange layman were on the other side of the desk. They all looked very solemn.

"Well, Alfredo," said the choirmaster, "the time has come for you to make an important choice. It is your decision you must make for yourself. It concerns your beautiful voice. The blessed Lord in his mercy and wisdom has decreed that at a certain age, which you will soon be reaching, the nature of the male body changes . . ."

And so on, for some while. Alfredo barely listened. He knew about the operation. He didn't care. All he wanted to do was sing. Nothing else mattered. When the choirmaster asked him if he had understood, he nodded. The choirmaster then introduced the stranger at the left of the line, who turned out to be the surgeon who would perform the operation. He told Alfredo about it, using long medical words that Alfredo certainly didn't understand, but when asked he again nodded impassively.

"So," said the choirmaster. "The choice is yours, Alfredo. Will you have the operation or not?"

"If it is your wish," said Alfredo listlessly. "Provided I can go on singing."

They looked at the fat little man behind the desk, who put the tips of his fingers together, pursed his lips and made a humming noise in the back of his throat to show he was thinking deeply.

"I think we may take that as willing consent," he said at last. "Yes, indeed, I think so."

He dipped a quill into his ink pot and started to write. The tension in the room relaxed.

There was a scratching at the door.

"Who is it?" said the Precentor irritably.

One of the vergers, Pietro, opened the door. Somebody was standing a pace behind him, a vague figure in the shadows.

"Beg pardon, Your Reverence," said Pietro. "This gentleman . . ."

But the gentleman in question had eased past him and was making a brief bow to the Precentor. He was a tall, elegant man, wigged, with a sword at his hip. He wore a brocade-trimmed gray dress coat, brown velvet breeches, white stockings and buckled shoes. His cravat was spotless white and he carried a tricorn hat under his left arm.

"The Cavalier Giorgio di Lucari, at your service, Holy Fathers," he said in a slow, hoarse voice, as if he found speaking difficult. "I bear a letter of introduction to His Eminence from my friend the Archbishop of Ravenna, but I gather His Eminence is not in town, and my mission is urgent. It concerns, I believe, this boy, my brother's son Alfredo."

With an elegant movement he placed a wax-sealed envelope on the desk.

After a moment of baffled silence the Precentor said, "Your brother's son, you say, sir? But the boy's patronymic is Benotti."

The gentleman sighed.

"Alas," he said. "My unfortunate brother, despite my most earnest pleading, chose to demean his ancient lineage by becoming a tradesman. But at least I prevailed upon him to spare the family honor so far as to change his name. I have no children, and the boy is my only heir. I have come posthaste, as soon as I heard of my brother's tragic death, to take the boy under my protection and bring him up in a manner proper to his inheritance."

There was another silence. The Precentor looked to his right, but the fat little man refused to meet his eye. Beyond him, Father Brava shrugged. The choirmaster coughed.

"The boy has just now chosen to become a full member of His Eminence's choir . . . ," he began, but the gentleman interrupted him. There was the touch of contempt now in the harshness of his voice.

"And this is the notary to engross the deed. And this, no doubt, is the surgeon to perform the operation. Fathers, I cannot permit it. The boy is the last of an ancient lineage. Would you snuff it out entirely, knowing that at the last day you shall stand before your maker and confess to such a deed?"

Yet another silence.

"In two days His Eminence will return . . . ," the Precentor suggested.

"Alas, I cannot wait," said the gentleman firmly. "I have affairs to conduct. If my poor brother did not appoint a guardian for the boy, then in law that task falls to me. My consent would be absolutely necessary for the operation, no matter what the boy himself has said. Is this not the case, sir?"

The fat little man jumped as if he had been stung.

"Yes . . . yes, I believe so," he said, with an apologetic grimace toward the Precentor.

"Well, I do not give it," said the gentleman firmly, then added, in a quieter tone, "But, Fathers, I gladly recognize the kindness of your intentions, and the generosity with which you have educated and trained my nephew, and in settlement of all such debts I am happy to make a reasonable payment to the cathedral, to be spent for the benefit of the choir, as you think fit."

He took a folded document from his breast pocket, opened it and laid it on the desk beside the envelope. The Precentor picked it up. His eyebrows rose as he studied it.

"That is indeed generous, sir," he said.

"My pleasure," said the gentleman. "Now I must be gone. I deeply regret that I am unable to have the pleasure of meeting His Eminence. You will give him my respects? If you need me, you will find me at the hostelry of St. Barnabas-by-the-Gate. Come, Alfredo."

He bowed once more, turned and left. Alfredo followed him numbly. Never to sing again! Never again!

There was a closed carriage waiting in the courtyard, of

the sort that plied for hire around the city. The gentleman opened the door and climbed in, Alfredo followed, and the horses trotted away toward the Northern Gate but, as soon as they were out of sight of the cathedral, swung left toward the harbor. The gentleman sat for a while, massaging his throat, and then opened a valise, which he had evidently left in the coach when he had come.

"Sit well back," he said. "Take that thing off and put this on. It will be small for you, but most boys grow faster than their parents can afford to reclothe them."

Still too numb to wonder what all this meant, Alfredo took off his ankle-length chorister's gown and worked his way into a coarse fustian overshirt, much like the one he used to wear at home. Meanwhile, the gentleman removed his wig, coat, stock, sword belt and shoes, pulled a pair of gray woollen stockings over his hose and replaced the other garments with ones much like those any prosperous shopkeeper or small merchant might have worn, going about his business. He folded his gentleman's outfit neatly and packed it into the valise, unscrewing the hilt from his sword to fit it in.

The coach stopped, they climbed out and the gentleman—gentleman now no longer—paid the coachman and led the way into the tangle of crowded streets above the harbor.

CHAPTER THREE

THREE HOURS LATER THEY WERE ON THE DECK OF a small boat watching the coastline dwindle behind them. After a while Alfredo's companion looked at his watch, drew a flask from an inner pocket and sipped slowly at it, throwing his head back to swallow, so that Alfredo saw the effort he found it to do so. All that time they had hardly exchanged a word, but now the man smiled a strange, bitter smile, without warmth or mirth.

"Thank you for asking no questions," he said in a grating whisper. "I have a constriction in my throat and must spare my voice, but the sea air is good for it, and my medicine helps for a while. Well, as you've probably guessed, I am not the Cavalier di Lucari, but I *am* your uncle Giorgio, and you may call me that. Aren't you going to say anything? I have just saved you from a painful operation and a lifetime of regret and shame. At some risk to myself, what's more. The penalty for forging a financial document is an extremely unpleasant death. You are not grateful?"

Alfredo looked up at him. He could feel tears starting to come.

"I'm sorry," he managed to say. "But I really wanted to sing. It's all I've got left."

"Poor boy," said Uncle Giorgio. "But it isn't all you have left. And you shall sing. Would you like to sing to me now? Not church music, I think. Do you know any songs of the sea?"

Alfredo cast his mind back to the old days and remembered a silly song he had picked up in the harbor long ago while Father was haggling with one of the merchants about a consignment of fine flour from the south. It was about a sailor numbering off the girls he had in the ports along the coast, adding a fresh name and port to the list with each verse. It had a pretty, lively tune, very far from how he was now feeling, but almost as soon as he'd started the music took over and he sang for the joy of singing.

Uncle Giorgio listened, smiling, and then reached out for Alfredo's neck.

"Don't stop," he said as his fingers felt beneath the collar, found the gold chain, pulled it free and gently lifted it over Alfredo's head and clear.

Alfredo's voice faltered. Something was badly wrong. He had to concentrate hard even to stay on the note, but his training held and he recovered himself and sang on. But for that moment the music had been empty, meaningless, and still there seemed to be a sort of inner uncertainty, until Uncle Giorgio replaced the chain and slid the little golden salamander back under Alfredo's shirt. The joy came back and Alfredo finished the song.

Shocked at last out of his apathy, he stared at his uncle.

"What . . . what happened?" he whispered.

"Originally there was no music in our own blood, Alfredo. All we have is the gift of the salamanders. They are intensely musical creatures. And we have known them long, very, very long, so that by now that gift of music has, as it were, bred itself into our family. It is, so to speak, our birthright. But it does not always run true. In a few of us it is manifest from the first. In some, such as your poor brother, it is entirely lacking. Your father had it, but—"

"But he couldn't sing at all! He was awful!"

Uncle Giorgio's voice grew even harsher.

"He chose not to, Alfredo. That was one of many bad choices."

"But . . ."

"Since you loved him, we had best not talk about it. What was I saying? . . . Yes, for most of us the gift is there, but needs the power of the salamanders to unlock it. If I had given your brother the pendant he might have sung, but not as you do. For you the pendant was, as it were, a key to unlock the casket that held your gift.

"And remember this. One thing I told those priests, at least, was true. We come of an extremely ancient lineage, you and I, older than that of any prince or cavalier you could name. And we two are the last of it. That is why I have risked my life to bring you away. I did not do it for your father's sake. I owe him nothing, nothing at all. You are very precious to me, Alfredo."

He chuckled, shaking his head. The dry, effortful whisper had made it impossible to guess at his feelings, but twice, when he'd been speaking of Father, there'd been something—and then the final chuckle . . . and for the first time Alfredo saw that Uncle Giorgio might be his father's brother. Must be. That was exactly how his father chuckled when he was pretending to make light of something that in fact really mattered to him . . . as on Alfredo's name-day almost four years ago. . . .

Yes, the brothers must have quarreled, and about something that had really mattered. ". . . *has no children, as far as I know . . .*" (that must have been Uncle Giorgio) "*. . . renounced my own birthright—I can't do that for him . . . make up his own mind . . .*" (and that must have been Alfredo himself).

But there'd been something that mattered even more, something that must have its Master. And because of that it was better for Alfredo to wear the salamander chain than not to. And Father had invited Uncle Giorgio to the christenings of both his sons.

And the neighbors had been right about Father's singing so badly. He'd been doing it on purpose.

"So we must make things up between us, as best we can," Uncle Giorgio went on. "It is proper that you should have loved your father, and I will not hold that against you. But now you have me in his place, and henceforth you will bear your true name, which is Alfredo di Sala. Are you content with that?"

Not knowing what to say, Alfredo nodded and waited to be told more, but Uncle Giorgio was massaging his throat in the way that he had in the coach, so Alfredo guessed it must be hurting because he had talked too much. Before long Uncle Giorgio went down to the cabin to rest, leaving Alfredo to sing softly, under his breath, hour after hour, while he watched the unchanging sea.

Next day they docked in a small harbor. Uncle Giorgio was evidently expected at the only inn, where another valise was waiting for him, and there was a mule in the stable ready to carry it and the rest of the baggage. They set out almost at once, up a steep track, but when they were well clear of the town Uncle Giorgio led the way to one side, halted as soon as they were hidden, opened the second valise and took out fresh clothes for the pair of them—a peasant's jacket and breeches for himself and a plain country smock for Alfredo, with wide-brimmed straw hats for both of them. They plodded on for the rest of afternoon along narrow tracks, rising and falling, supped and slept in a deserted hut far up a hillside and journeyed on next day, coming late that afternoon to a final crest above a different harbor town. They neared its walls a little before sunset, but before they reached it, turned aside once more. In a tumbledown shack Uncle Giorgio changed back into his merchant's dress.

"Wait here," he croaked. "Bell rings before gates close. Go through when others go. Harbor. Largest boat at quay—*Bonaventura*—go below. Cabin. Wait for me."

He took the mule's bridle and strode on toward the town.

Alfredo was not worried to be left alone. By now he understood what was happening. His uncle had pretended to be a rich gentleman in order to impress the priests, and then had effectively bought Alfredo from them with what seemed to be a generous donation to the choir, though no doubt they planned to keep most of it for themselves. Without that they might have argued, made difficulties until the Prince-Cardinal returned. If *he* wished to keep Alfredo in the choir, it barely mattered what the law said. But the donation was of course worthless, the letter of introduction probably a blank sheet of paper. The Prince-Cardinal would be outraged, and if Uncle Giorgio was caught he would face a horrible death. So he was covering their tracks, pretending to be still at the hostelry of St. Barnabas when he had already left the city, changing their clothes, taking this roundabout but already prepared route home and now, at this new harbor, concealing Alfredo's existence in the hope of smuggling him out to sea unnoticed.

Alfredo did as he was told, slipping in through the gates in the dusk among a group of latecomers and then finding his way to the harbor. There was no mistaking the *Bonaventura*. A sailor, leaning on the farther rail, glanced round as the gangplank creaked beneath Alfredo's weight, raised a hand and returned to his contemplation of the harbor. Alfredo climbed down the companionway. In the pitch darkness of the well, lines of light gleamed around a door. He opened it and found that the light came from a lantern slung from a cabin ceiling. Uncle Giorgio's valises were on the floor. He took off his boots, lay down in one of the two hammocks and once again waited.

He was asleep when Uncle Giorgio arrived, bringing a wicker basket with an excellent cold meal for Alfredo: fish salad, oil, good coarse bread, apricots and rough red wine. He himself ate nothing, but sipped slowly from a pot of what smelled like chicken broth, and drank a little wine, swallowing with obvious difficulty.

"Aren't you going to have any?" said Alfredo. "It's very good."

Uncle Giorgio shook his head and simply pointed at his throat. He took his flask out of his pocket, weighed it in his hand and put it back. He reached down and from a pocket in his valise took out three similar flasks, which he unstoppered and stood on the table. He poured a dribble of wine into each, swilled it round and sipped it slowly.

"It was kind of you to get it for me," said Alfredo. "Thank you very much."

Uncle Giorgio nodded, unsmiling. Yes, it had been kind of him. It was proper that Alfredo should recognize the fact. Alfredo still didn't know what to make of his uncle. There was so much that reminded him of Father: his erect stance and long, stiff stride; the way he drummed the fingers of his right hand on his left wrist as he thought; the way he preferred to sit sideways on at the table while he ate, and would then rise sidelong from his chair—small things, but so like in both men. With Uncle Giorgio barely able to speak it was harder to tell about the big things, but in spite of his apparent kindness—from the huge risk he was taking for Alfredo's sake to his consideration in bringing a pleasant meal to the cabin, though he himself couldn't eat any of it—there was one big difference. Father had *loved*—loved his family, loved his baking, loved other people, loved life. Even in his angers there had been love. Even if his throat had been hurting, the way Uncle Giorgio's was . . . No, that wasn't fair. And in any case, Alfredo wouldn't have wanted Uncle Giorgio, well or ill, to be just like Father, would he?

"Is your throat very sore?" he asked.

Uncle Giorgio nodded, expressionless.

"Would you like me to sing for you?"

Uncle Giorgio shook his head, pointed toward the quay and cupped a hand behind his ear. *No, not now. People might hear you. We are trying to hide you.*

Alfredo nodded to show he'd understood, but was inwardly puzzled. What about the sailor who'd seen him board? How much could Uncle Giorgio have paid to buy the silence of the whole crew? Perhaps this wasn't the *Bonaventura*'s home port. . . .

The puzzle deepened as the days went by. They had sailed at dawn on that first morning, heading almost due into the rising sun. Uncle Giorgio spent all day on deck, breathing the sea air to ease his throat. When Alfredo had asked if he should come up too he had just nodded. Two sailors rigged a hammock for him, and Alfredo sat on a coil of rope beside him. Uncle Giorgio produced an old book from a pocket, opened it and pointed at a page before passing it to Alfredo. It was a psalter, in Latin of course, with a plainsong notation for each psalm. The book was open at Psalm 137, *Super flumina Babylonis.*

"This chant, Uncle Giorgio?" asked Alfredo, showing the book.

Raised eyebrows—*What else do you suggest?*

"There's one of the cathedral ones. Most of them . . ."

The nod—*Yes*—interrupted him. He'd been going to explain that he knew several settings—the psalm was popular with composers—but only one that was suitable for a single treble voice, a prolonged descant continuing through the whole setting above the intertwining voices of the choir, but beautiful in its own right. As a junior until this year he had never got to sing it, in fact had heard it only twice, but both times had silently sung it through in his mind for hours after the service had ended. One day, he had promised himself, he would sing it aloud for the Prince-Cardinal. Instead he was singing it for a sick man, and perhaps a few sailors if they cared to listen, on the deck of a small boat out on the open sea. But he sang it with his whole heart, as he would have in the cathedral. It was music. It was all he had left, still.

"By the waters of Babylon I sat down and wept, when I remembered thee, O Sion . . ."

The sailors did indeed listen. Three of the four stopped their work to do so—the fourth was the helmsman. There were calls of *"Bravo!"* *"Bravissimo!"* when he finished. Uncle Giorgio merely nodded approval. Alfredo leafed back a few pages to another favorite. *"I will lift up mine eyes unto the hills,"* he sang, though the setting was not quite so good for a single voice. He was about to look for another one when Uncle Giorgio stopped him with a gesture, looked up at the sun, then at his watch, rose, but staggered as the boat heaved to the swell and would have fallen if a sailor hadn't caught his elbow and helped him aft.

Alfredo watched the confrontation with the helmsman. It began calmly enough. From Uncle Giorgio's gestures he wanted the boat to head farther south. The helmsman shook his head and spoke briefly. Uncle Giorgio became more vehement. The helmsman held his course. Uncle Giorgio seized his arm. The helmsman shoved him away, handed the helm to one of the other men and yelled at Uncle Giorgio that he was the captain of this #!?#!! boat and no #!?#!! passenger was going to tell him how to mind his ship, no matter how much #!?#!! money he'd paid to smuggle his fancy boy off the island, and if Uncle Giorgio didn't like it he'd turn the boat right round and take him back where he'd come from and the hell with the money. Voice like that, there'd be somebody who'd pay as much to get the boy back.

To show he meant what he said he dug into his breeches pocket, pulled out a small canvas bag and flung it on the deck at Uncle Giorgio's feet.

Uncle Giorgio stared at him, his face set and pale as bone. Alfredo could actually feel his fury, its need to burst out, engulf, destroy, in the same kind of way that he had been able to feel a surge in one of the oven fire pits when a sudden shift of wind increased the draft in the flue, feel it and close the dampers long before the extra heat could seep through into the oven, or the bakehouse. So now. Alfredo watched and felt Uncle Giorgio grimly applying his own inward dampers as he turned away. The sailor helped him back to the hammock. The ship sailed on, due east.

That afternoon Uncle Giorgio managed to doze for a while. One of the sailors was splicing a cable, whistling as he worked, a tune Alfredo didn't know. When he went to listen the sailor looked up, and stopped whistling.

"What's with the old boy, then?" he asked. "Skipper's got a short fuse, but the rule is, never speak to the man at the wheel, leave alone grab hold of him. Even a landsman should've known that."

"He's sick," explained Alfredo. "His throat's very bad, and he's running out of his medicine. He's got much worse since we left. . . . He hasn't told me, but if he doesn't get more medicine soon I think he might die. That's why he's desperate to get, er, home."

He had hesitated because he still had no idea where they were going. If it was "home," it would still be strange to him. The sailor appeared not to notice, but unconsciously answered the question for him.

"Well then," he said, pointing to the right of their course, just as Uncle Giorgio had done. "Sicily's that way, five days in the right wind, which this isn't. Lot of tacking, it'd mean. So skipper's heading for the mainland, and then he'll turn along the coast and we'll have the shore breezes all the way to the Straits, and a lot less tacking. Get there quicker in the end. You tell the old boy that."

"How long will it take this way?"

"Seven, eight days. Or we could pull in at Ostia, say, and get him some medicine there. Laudanum would be better than nothing, I'd have said—stop it hurting so bad."

"How long would that take?"

"Putting in for the stuff and then getting back on course? Better part of a morning, maybe. You ask him about that, and I'll have a word with the skipper, tell him what the hurry is. He'll do his best. He's not the type to hold a grudge."

Before he could return to his splicing Alfredo asked him about the tune he'd been whistling. It was a popular drinking song, which he sang for Alfredo in a wheezy tenor, and Alfredo then sang it back to him, ornamenting the chorus as he went. They laughed together when he'd finished and Alfredo went back to Uncle Giorgio and told him what the sailor had said. After that he read to him from a Latin book called *Arcana Ignea,* which seemed to be about using fire to turn things into other things, but was full of strange words Alfredo didn't understand.

Uncle Giorgio lay and listened with closed eyes until the skipper came over and rather stiffly told Uncle Giorgio that he was now making the best speed he could, and offered to put in at Ostia for laudanum. Uncle Giorgio took out his watch, tapped it with his forefinger and firmly shook his head.

No. I cannot spare the time.

The passage took eight days. Benno, the sailor Alfredo had talked to, told him that on their usual trading voyages up and down the coast they preferred not to sail in the dark, so they anchored every night if they could; but now they were keeping watches and sailing on. The wind held and the weather was fine. The fourth day was a Sunday, and at Benno's request Alfredo sang church music for them, the part of Psalm 107 about ships in a storm, though of course he couldn't get the full tumultuous effect with only his single voice. By now all five of the crew had become solicitous for Uncle Giorgio's health—not only for his sake, Alfredo guessed. It would be most unlucky to have him die on board. In the evenings, when both watches were on deck for supper, they would hold concerts for him, Alfredo singing treble, Benno and one of the others tenor, the captain a fine baritone and the fourth sailor fancying himself as a bass.

Uncle Giorgio listened unsmiling, and at the end acknowledged their efforts with a nod, as he did when anything else was done for him. He never complained or showed any sign of impatience. He endured.

CHAPTER FOUR

In the dawn of the eighth morning Benno took Alfredo up to the bow and pointed. To their left lay the landmass of Italy, as it had all along, but now it seemed to curve round, blocking their path. Straight ahead, outlined against the pallid dawn sky, stood a mountain, a single flattened cone, from whose point rose a thin plume of smoke, drifting east away on the wind.

"Etna," said Benno. "Bloody great fire inside it, Alfredo. Bursts out sometimes. You don't want to be anywhere near it when it does that."

Alfredo stared. Yes, he realized; already, before he had seen it, even in his last dreams of the night, he had been vaguely conscious of that monstrous furnace, nearing.

All morning the mountain came closer and grew huger. Now Alfredo, if he closed his eyes, seemed able to trace through the layers of rock around them the channels of fiery matter that fed the smoking cauldron at the peak; and he could sense too, though much more vaguely, the immeasurable mass of fire below, a furnace the size of the turning world. He was both enthralled and terrified.

This morning Uncle Giorgio didn't ask to be sung to, but with signs got the sailors to re-sling his hammock so that he too could watch the mountain. He had been growing steadily weaker; swallowing gruel or wine was a painful struggle; each breath he took ended with a rasping croak. "You will get him home and then he will die," Benno had whispered yesterday. "That is something. It's better to die at home." But this morning Uncle Giorgio seemed a little stronger.

By noon they were sailing through a strait between Italy and what Benno said was the island of Sicily. The mainland receded on their left and the coast continued on their right. There the mountain soared, rising directly from the sea. In midafternoon they landed at a small harbor at its foot.

Alfredo said good-bye to the crew. Uncle Giorgio paid the captain, counting out several gold coins, and walked slowly but erect down the gangplank, but from there on leaned heavily on Alfredo's shoulder, croaking with the effort of each step. Two of the crew followed with the baggage. They reached an inn where Uncle Giorgio seemed to be known, not as a friend, but as a grand person to be treated with deference. If anything, they seemed a bit scared of him. While he sat and rested in the courtyard they brought him wine and olives, which he left untouched. Two mules were led out to be saddled and harnessed. One was loaded with the baggage, and Uncle Giorgio was helped—lifted, really—onto a mounting block and thence onto the back of the other. Alfredo took the halter of the pack mule and they started up a lane that soon became a many-branching track between the vineyards that covered the lower slopes of the mountain.

Alfredo climbed in a daze, half stunned by the nearness of the central fires. He had no idea where they were going, and Uncle Giorgio sat with his head bowed and the reins slack, by sheer willpower forcing his body to last out this final stage of the dreadful journey. But the mules seemed to know the way and plodded steadily on. Now they were sidling up a spur. On the ridge Uncle Giorgio seemed to drag himself up from his trance of endurance, reining his mule back and turning it off the track. With a gesture to Alfredo to stay where he was, he headed up between two rows of vines, halted some distance into the vineyard and stared out to sea. Alfredo turned to see what he was looking at.

It was a stupendous view. This side of the mountain was now in shadow. So were the orange roofs of the harbor, but the sea beyond, though hazy with heat in the distance, glittered and dazzled. Toy boats dotted the busy sea-lane. Which of them was the *Bonaventura*? There—with the yellow patch on the brown sail. Would they still have concerts each evening, Benno happily wheezing, the captain holding the others steady, the bass booming mellowly, but erratic on the note? What did they really think of their two curious passengers, the dying merchant and the choirboy? Uncle Giorgio had evidently paid them well, to buy their silence as well as their passage, but how could he rely on them once they were no longer under his eye? Benno, in particular, was a chatterbox. . . .

Something was happening inside the mountain, a surge, a change. The hairs on Alfredo's neck stirred as his whole skin crawled. It was coming . . . ! No, not here . . . Farther . . . There! Oh, Mother of Jesus!

The *Bonaventura* exploded into flame, the flames themselves invisible in the sunlight but the smoke surging suddenly upward in dense, churning bulges, renewed and renewed from below as the breeze thinned and scattered them. Alfredo stared, aghast, stunned, unable to think or feel. All he could do was stare at the smoke of the burning vessel as it rose in dark masses above the silky water.

A shod hoof clicked on shale behind him.

Slowly, still too numb to grasp what had happened, he turned and watched his uncle coming down between the vines. He had let go of the reins and was sitting bowed and swaying, grasping the pommel of the saddle to hold himself in place. As he reached the path the fury of the mountain seemed to recede. Alfredo felt its fires quieten beneath his feet.

Unguided, Uncle Giorgio's mule turned on up the path. Alfredo's mule started to follow. The tug on his arm from the reins broke the trance. Feeling returned—shock, grief, horror, terror—overwhelming thought. Terror was strongest. He turned to run, to race back down to the harbor and beg for a passage on the first boat leaving. But the halter was wound round his hand and dragged him back as the mule plodded on up the path, forcing him to follow until he could slacken it enough to free himself. He cast a despairing look out to sea as he stumbled and struggled, and now at last remembered that even there he wouldn't be safe—hadn't he seen what happened to the *Bonaventura*? And as the distance between him and Uncle Giorgio increased, he seemed to sense the inexplicable angers of the mountain gathering themselves to strike again, as if the only safety for him lay within his uncle's protection. With a violent shudder he pulled himself together and hurried to catch up.

Soon they left the vineyards behind and climbed among ancient gray olive trees, with rough grass beneath them, until they reached a stone wall, higher than a man, stretching along the hillside. The mules turned left, rounded a corner and climbed a steep ramp to an upper level. Here Alfredo discovered that the wall had been built to retain a wide terrace, at the back of which stood a long, low house with a densely wooded slope beyond. The house was large but shabby, with mottled and peeling cream-colored walls beneath the wide eaves of a wavy-tiled orange roof. To one side of it a man was listlessly hoeing.

At the sound of hooves he looked up, stared slack-jawed and with a strange bubbling cry rushed out of sight round the corner of the house. The mules began to follow him, but at the next corner of the house they were met by a woman in peasant clothes—tall, gaunt, skin brown as the leather of a boot—who without a word of greeting seized the bridle of Uncle Giorgio's mule, turned it and led it back the way they had come. The man came creeping behind, clearly ready to scuttle away again.

The woman halted at the front door and tapped on Uncle Giorgio's knee. He let go of the pommel and simply tumbled into her arms. She was as strong as a strong man, took his weight easily, settled him on his feet, drew his arm round her shoulder and put hers round his waist and half-led, half-carried him into the house. At the door she turned and signed to Alfredo to follow.

Alfredo hesitated. The house, the woman, the man, the homecoming itself seemed unbearably scary and strange. But he thought he could feel the mountain watching him, and he was certain that however fast he ran it would have the power to reach out with a tongue of flame and between pace and pace turn him to ashes. Leaving the man to cope with the mules, he numbly followed the others into the house.

They were waiting for him on the far side of an empty stone-flagged hall. The woman picked up a lit lantern and gave it to Alfredo. She helped Uncle Giorgio on through an archway into a dark passage, and then slowly and carefully down a steep ladder-like stair. At the bottom was an even darker passage. She turned right. They passed several openings—cellars and storerooms, Alfredo saw as they were briefly lit by the lantern. The passage ended in a heavy iron door. Uncle Giorgio pulled a large key from an inner pocket and gave it to the woman. She beckoned to Alfredo to take her place, then unlocked the door, pushed it open, handed the key back to Uncle Giorgio and stood aside. Leaning heavily on Alfredo, Uncle Giorgio dragged himself into the room.

It was a vaulted chamber, wider than the bakehouse at home, but with a low roof supported by a pair of pillars. In the dimness around the walls Alfredo could see book-shelves, shelves of jars, the gleam of brass vessels and pipes, and what looked like a fiddle in its case. In the center of the room, between the pillars, stood something like the bottom section of a much larger pillar, a bulky brick cylinder with an iron lid. Though no heat came from it, and the chamber felt no warmer than the passage they'd left, Alfredo knew at once what lay beneath that lid. Fire. A compact mass of pure heat, somehow contained within the cylinder, not radiating at all. It was so strange that for a little while he forgot his terror and simply stared as they drew nearer.

They reached it and Uncle Giorgio let go of Alfredo, propped himself with one arm on the brickwork and with the other reached shakily out and with his bare hand grasped the handle. It was beyond his strength to lift the lid. Alfredo moved round and held his open palm a little above the metal. Still no heat. Cautiously he took hold of the handle. It was faintly warm. He started to heave the lid up and at once his eyes screwed shut of their own accord rather than face the blast of light that struck them. Light like the light of the sun, but with as little heat as that of the moon. There was no smoke, no odor of fire at all. Yet the heat was there, though somehow it stopped at the surface, so that even on bare flesh he couldn't feel it at all. But it struck and almost overwhelmed his inward senses, more intense than anything he had known or imagined, heat from the heart of the sun.

He turned his face away but even then could barely open his eyes. The room blazed with light, flinging shadows as intensely black. Uncle Giorgio was beckoning impatiently. Alfredo's fear returned as he edged back round the glaring crucible. Had he been brought here to be fed into the furnace, a sacrifice to the fire, which would then somehow magically heal Uncle Giorgio's throat? No, Uncle Giorgio had a book in his hands—the psalter—but they were shaking too badly for him to turn the pages as he wanted. He let Alfredo take it from him and find the place. Alfredo had known without asking. Psalm 137, *Super flumina*. He showed it to Uncle Giorgio, who nodded. Alfredo turned, closed his eyes, drew a breath, steadied himself and sang to the fire.

Fire that Father had so loved, and taught him to love; fire that had taken away all that he had loved, his parents, his brother, his home, even the *Bonaventura*, everything except the act of singing. His grief, his loss, his anguish, welled into the music, welled into words that were already there to take it:

By the waters of Babylon we sat down and wept, when we remembered thee, O Sion.
As for our harps, we hanged them up upon the trees that are therein.
For they that led us away captive required of us a song, and melody in our heaviness: "Sing us one of the songs of Sion."
How shall we sing the Lord's song in a strange land? . . .

He paused, because there was a three-bar rest for the descant at that point in the setting, but another voice sang on, wordless, a full octave higher than his own highest reach, but sweeter and truer than the best voice in the choir.

Startled, he opened his eyes. Uncle Giorgio, wearing spectacles now, their lenses densest black, was leaning forward, stretching an arm out over the surface of the crucible, holding a small ladle. Something had changed at the center of the glare, too bright for Alfredo to make out, or even to look at for more than an instant. He closed his eyes and rejoined the music two bars late. It didn't matter. The other voice was ready, eager for his coming. In an exultation of sorrow the two of them sang through to the end. When he opened his eyes again, the glaring surface was just as it had been when he had first seen it. Whatever had been in the midst of it was gone. Uncle Giorgio signaled to him to close the lid.

After that fierce light the chamber was blackness for a while, despite the glow from the lantern. By the time Alfredo could see, Uncle Giorgio was sitting in the chair, holding the little ladle in his left hand and a small glass syringe in his right. With trembling fingers he dipped the nozzle of the syringe into the bowl of the ladle and sucked out the contents. He tilted his head back and raised the syringe. Alfredo could see the liquid through the glass, just a few drops, golden in the lamplight. Uncle Giorgio squeezed them one by one into the back of his throat. He closed his eyes, bowed his head and sat motionless. Alfredo heard the sawing rasp of his breath, once, twice, three times, but less each time and then silent. He waited, too dazed with the wonder of the singing, his own voice and the other, double but single in the song, for either terror or amazement.

After a while Uncle Giorgio looked up, drew a deep breath, rose and stretched as if he'd just woken from deep sleep.

"The tears of the salamander," he said in a voice like any other man's, only a little husky. "The ichor of the sun. Sovereign against all ailments of the flesh.

"And at last, Alfredo, I can welcome you to Casa di Sala. My home, and now yours."

CHAPTER FIVE

Alfredo sat on the window seat in his room, gazing out at the night. *His* room—Uncle Giorgio had said so, showing him in. It was large—larger than his parents' had been, above the bakehouse—with a bed big enough for five, and some heavy dark old furniture. In the back of the closet Alfredo had found a small chest, empty apart from a few schoolbooks. The one he opened had the initials A.V.DI S. inside the front cover. The first two were the same as his own—Alfredo Vittorio . . . No! All three were the same as his own, now—Alfredo Vittorio di Sala. Impossible. The books were old, with underlinings and doodles in the margins. No again, not impossible. Antonio Vittorio di Sala—Father's name once. This room must have been Father's room, long ago.

He had stood and stared round it, aching with longing for some whisper of a voice, the ghost of a footfall, a presence, however faint. Nothing. The ache still filled him now as he sat—how often his father must have done the same—staring out at the soft calm night, smelling the sweet calm odors. He *needed* Father. Father had filled his life. The world was empty without him. Now, Father would have told him what to do, what to think, what to believe, as dread wrestled with amazed excitement in his mind. And all the time he could sense, through the deep layers of rock behind his back and beneath his feet the implacable fiery power of the mountain.

They had climbed back up from the cellars and the silent woman had brought them supper in a small room that seemed only to be used for eating. The food was peasant stuff, but excellent and plentiful, and the forks and spoons were silver, well polished, and there were fine white napkins. Uncle Giorgio ate in silence, as if eating were all that mattered to him in the world. He filled his plate three times, taking small mouthfuls and chewing them well but swallowing without difficulty. Alfredo felt too tense to eat but was too hungry not to, so chewed and swallowed, barely noticing the taste. When they had finished, Uncle Giorgio pushed his chair back and looked at Alfredo for the first time since they had sat down.

"I am too tired for questions," he said. "I have been very near death. I miscalculated. It is a long time since I was away from here for more than a few days. I was aware that the tears of the salamander begin to lose their virtue once they are shed, but I did not guess by how much. Is there anything you need to know now?"

"Someone . . . something sang . . . in the . . . I don't know what to call it. . . ."

Uncle Giorgio smiled for almost the first time since Alfredo had known him.

"In the furnace?" he said. "That was my salamander. It

answered your singing and wept for me, so that I could drink its tears and be healed. Is there anything else?"

"The . . . the *Bonaventura* . . . it wasn't ordinary fire. The mountain did something. I felt it," said Alfredo.

Uncle Giorgio sighed and shook his head sadly.

"Yes, it is in your blood to feel it," he said at last. "The mountain destroyed the ship in vengeance for its having brought me back. I am the Master of the Mountain, as our ancestors have been for more than a thousand years, and in full health I could have restrained it. I did what I could, but to my grief I was too feeble. That is my task, to control the rages of the mountain. One day it will be yours. I will tell you more tomorrow."

And that had been all.

So Alfredo sat at his window while the night wheeled on, trying to think about the salamander, and the mountain, and his uncle. Master of the Mountain! Yes, that was what Father had been saying on the evening of his name-day. "*The Mountain must have its Master. . . .*" It had been an extraordinary relief to have even that little explained, however strange the explanation.

And it didn't even feel all that strange to Alfredo. In fact, it felt somehow *familiar*—something he hadn't known but had, so to speak, been all along waiting to know. . . . And in the same way the terrible thing that had happened to the *Bonaventura* made sense to him since Uncle Giorgio had explained it.

He thought about Uncle Giorgio—how like he was to Father, and how different. When Father had smiled you could feel how pleased he was. When he had sighed you shared his sadness. His feelings beamed out of him, like the heat from his ovens. But Uncle Giorgio was like the salamander's furnace—there were great fiery energies inside him—Alfredo was sure of that—but they stopped at the surface. You couldn't feel them, not in his smile, not in his sigh.

His thoughts went round and round, until he fell asleep where he sat. He woke in the dawn chilled through, though the fire of the mountain had raged through his dreams. He crept shuddering into the bed, *his* bed, and fell asleep again, this time with no dreams, and didn't wake until the sun was high. And still he didn't know what to do or think or feel. There was food in the eating room—bread, fruit, oil, dried fish, water flavored with lime. He was eating with furious hunger when the silent woman came in, nodded and left. She returned a little later and simply stood waiting. Her presence was uncomfortable, so Alfredo pushed his plate away unfinished and rose.

"Please, where is my uncle?" he asked hesitantly.

For answer the woman opened her mouth and pointed her finger into it, shaking her head as she did so. She then beckoned to him to follow her. The room where they ate was down a side passage at one end of a wide corridor that ran the full length of the house. The woman led him along this, past the hallway and the stairs and then down another side passage. At the far end of this she scratched on a door, waited for an answer, then opened the door and held it for him.

Inside Alfredo found a fair-sized room. One window looked toward the mountain, invisible behind woods.

Outside the other one the trees stood closer, almost brushing the panes. Uncle Giorgio was working at a desk, apparently copying something out of a thick book. He glanced up and nodded to the woman. She left, closing the door, and Uncle Giorgio returned to his writing. Alfredo gazed round the room. Apart from the two windows, every inch of the walls was covered with shelves, most of them filled with books, but the ones at the farther end held dozens of labeled jars and flasks, like those in a pharmacist's shop. There was a long table with glass and brass apparatus on it, delicate scales and small implements. Beside that stood a small brazier, unlit. Above it, hanging from a hook in the ceiling, was a birdcage, containing what looked like a starling.

The bird seemed to notice that Alfredo was looking at it and eyed him back, cocking its head a little to one side.

"One! Two! Three! Four!" it screeched suddenly. And again "One! Two! Three! Four!"

Alfredo jumped at the harsh, inhuman cry and the unmistakably human words. Uncle Giorgio wiped his quill and laid it down, sanded his paper, closed the book, marking the page with a scrap of paper, and rose.

"One! Two! Three! Four!" shrieked the starling as he took a crust of bread from a bag hanging on a peg and wedged it between the bars of the cage. The starling fell on it.

"A reward for speech," said Uncle Giorgio.

"Can it say anything else?"

"There is no need. Come with me."

He led the way down to the cellars and along to the

furnace room. This time he took a second pair of the black-lensed spectacles from his pocket and gave them to Alfredo.

"I made these for you before you woke," he said. "Wear them always before I open the crucible, or it will destroy your eyesight. Stand well back, but be ready to sing the psalm when I tell you."

Alfredo put the spectacles on and could see nothing. The glass seemed totally opaque, but as soon as Uncle Giorgio raised the lid of the crucible the glare struck through, as strong as that of the glowing embers in the fire pit of one of the bakehouse ovens, but now bearable. The fierce orange surface was as smooth as liquid but didn't boil or churn, even when Uncle Giorgio, using tongs, fed it with two or three dark lumps, too heavy to be charcoal. They might have been pit coal, but didn't look like that, either, and didn't smoke or crackle, despite the intense heat immediately below the surface. Instead they settled slowly into it and sank out of sight.

"Stand still farther back," said Uncle Giorgio. "This fire is the fire of the inmost sun. It sends out an emanation that alters the nature of the flesh, making it cancerous, as has happened in my own throat. Good. Now sing."

Fear and excitement dried Alfredo's mouth. His whole body seemed to be fluttering like the air in the bass pipes of the cathedral organ. He wasn't sure he could sing at all—there would be none of the usual joy in it—but he sucked and swallowed two or three times, pulled himself together and almost listlessly began.

Before he was through the first bar of the music the fiery

surface rippled and the salamander emerged. He could see it clearly through the dark glass of his spectacles. It rose until it was waist deep in the liquid, and then stopped. Its body rippled with the flow of heat, like a burning ember. Apart from the flattish oval of its face it was covered with neat triangular scales. Its eyes were round and slightly pop, and of a black unimaginably deep, full of living fire, like the rest of it—but fire that gave out no light at all. Instead the eyes sucked light into their own blackness. The creature had human-seeming ears but no nose. There were flaps on either side of its neck, like the gills of a fish. Its mouth was a small, round, lipless hole, which widened only a little as it started to answer Alfredo's singing. The flaps on its neck pulsed gently.

As the first pure, high phrase twined itself in with Alfredo's, his whole mood changed. All his doubt and fear became longing, all his excitement became love. He knew in that instant that he had found a friend. He and the salamander spoke to each other as if they had known each other since time began. The music was their language, whose notes were words. Alfredo needed the actual words of the psalm only to give him something to sing, to embody the notes. The salamander needed no words at all.

They spoke, as new-made friends do, mainly about themselves, who they were and where they came from. The salamander took Alfredo into the heart of the mountain, into the fiery caverns through which flowed the streams of molten rock in which the salamanders swam, or hauled themselves out onto the glowing ledges to sing. The whole mountain rang with their singing. It was their life, their reason for existence, that they should sing to each other. It was the loss of that that filled the salamander with such longing. So intense was the sung friendship that Alfredo saw and knew and felt these things, as if he himself had lived as a salamander.

He, not in his turn but at the self-same time, took the salamander home. He took it into the bakehouse where the three ovens Father had built beamed out their inner heat as the rich loaves rose — a pale, faint heat, compared to that of the mountain, but still born of the living fire. He took it into the kitchen, where the family sat round their Sunday supper, content in their love for each other. He took it singing up through the twisting street into the glimmering darkness of the cathedral, where eight hundred lit candles glowed for the evening Mass, and the choir processed to their stalls and there sang their sweetest for the glory of God and the delight of the Prince-Cardinal.

Both boy and salamander wept.

Through the blur of his tears Alfredo was mistily aware of Uncle Giorgio leaning over the furnace, with his little ladle in his gloved hand, to catch the drops that fell from the salamander's cheeks. Then the psalm ended, the salamander withdrew below the surface, Uncle Giorgio closed the lid, and Alfredo was left with the echoes of the music dwindling in his mind.

He removed his spectacles and wiped his eyes on his sleeve. By the time he could see clearly, Uncle Giorgio was stoppering a little flask. He slipped it into a pocket, gazed impassively down at Alfredo for several seconds, shook his head as if in reproof, and picked up a strange little dish. It was shaped like one of the bakehouse loaf tins, but would have baked only one small finger-roll, and had a long handle and was made of iron. Carefully Uncle Giorgio wiped its inner surface with a greasy rag.

"Watch," he commanded.

Crouching beside him, Alfredo saw him reach with both hands beneath the furnace and turn a spigot. A thin stream of golden liquid flowed out into the pan. When it was almost full Uncle Giorgio closed the spigot, rose and set the pan down.

"Pure gold," he said calmly.

He fetched a second pan, crouched again, half-filled it and set it beside the first.

"Today we will climb the mountain," he said, and led the way out.

The track was much steeper than the one they had climbed between the vineyards, but the mules scrambled up it surefooted. The one Alfredo was riding wasn't the one he'd led up the mountain. Like Uncle Giorgio, he sat sideways in the saddle. They had broad-brimmed straw hats slung behind their shoulders, but for a long while didn't need to wear them as the path wound up through the shade of dense old woodland. Uncle Giorgio didn't say a word. Alfredo clung swaying to the saddle. The doubt and dread of yesterday's climb from the harbor had returned, and became stronger all the time as the layers of rock below him thinned and he felt himself drawn nearer and nearer to the central furnace.

It was well past noon when the woods abruptly gave way to a seemingly endless slope of dark gray tumbled boulders, shale and ash. Uncle Giorgio dismounted and Alfredo slid thankfully down. In the last of the shade they tethered the mules and settled down to the luncheon basket that the dumb woman had prepared for them.

They ate in silence. Alfredo was at first almost overwhelmed by his closeness to the churning fires below, in the heart of the mountain, but by the time he was packing the remains of the meal into the saddlebags he was even more conscious of Uncle Giorgio's steady, absorbed gaze on him.

There had been priests in the cathedral who might stare at you with the same intentness, but Uncle Giorgio's look was somehow different. That wasn't what he wanted, whatever the sailors on the *Bonaventura* might have thought. He and Alfredo had slept in the same cabins all through the voyage, traveled together through lonely woods and across empty hillsides, but he'd never once done or said anything to suggest any physical interest in his nephew. It was as if there was something else he wanted, deeply and passionately wanted, and only Alfredo could give it to him. But Alfredo had no idea what it was.

He closed the last buckle and stood waiting, but Uncle Giorgio made no move.

"Sit down," he said. "It is too hot to climb."

Again Alfredo sat. The mules fidgeted. Insects hazed through the mottled shade.

"There are two Great Works," said Uncle Giorgio

suddenly. "They are named the Philosophers' Stone and the Elixir of Life. Great men have sought them through the ages. With the Stone they hoped to achieve the transmutation of metals, and thus turn lead into gold. With the Elixir they hoped to live forever. They worked by the distillation of acids and the decoction and sublimation of minerals, and by the conjuration of demons, and achieved many things, but not their goals. These cannot be reached by such means.

"Where is gold found, Alfredo? It is found in the veins of rocks, rocks that once were molten in the heart of mountains such as this. It is found in streams, which have worn those rocks away. All substances, however chill, have fire locked within them. It is not the fire at which we warm our hands on a winter night, or use to cook our food. It is fire from the heart of the sun, which is more, even, than the fire that fills our turning world, and fills this mountain. In it live the salamanders. They take the gross materials of which all things are made and feed upon that inner fire. Heat is generated in the process, enough to turn the molten rock from the mountain, with which I originally filled my furnace, into true sun-stuff. The salamanders pass the rest through their bodies, so that it emerges changed. Some of it is transmuted into gold. Being heavy, the gold that my salamander makes sinks to the bottom of the furnace. But in the mountains it gathers together in pools and rivulets, so that when those places are churned to the surface and cool and become rocks, there are veins of gold running through them.

"Only the salamanders can turn lead to gold. That knowledge is the First Great Work, and I have accomplished it."

He fell silent, still watching Alfredo with the same heavy gaze, but now as if he expected some response. Alfredo nerved himself to return the look. Uncle Giorgio's eyebrows rose.

"Are you going to live forever?" Alfredo asked.

"Perhaps," said Uncle Giorgio, then paused and added, smiling his strange, unpracticed smile, "So, perhaps, will you."

Before the heat of the day was anything like over, they started on up the slope. Now they truly needed their hats, as they climbed between two fires, that of the mountain below and that of the sun above. Even in the shade of his broad straw brim Alfredo could feel the roasting power of the sun beamed back from the gray litter of old eruptions. If he lifted his head to see how far they still had to go to the summit, the glare at once blinded him. He felt as if they were toiling up into the sun itself, into the true home of the salamanders.

The heat from above was steady and relentless, but that from below varied. Sometimes he was shielded from it by layer upon layer of solid rock. At other times it ran so close to the surface that he felt that Uncle Giorgio, if he had chosen, could with a snap of his fingers have caused it to burst out at their feet.

The feeling was no longer frightening. If anything, there was an exhilaration in being so close to the source of such power. The only thing he had known that was at all like it was standing in his place in the choir with his breath ready drawn for the first full note while he watched for the downbeat of the Precentor's right hand, telling him to begin. Both the cathedral and this barren, heat-blasted summit were places where he belonged.

The mules climbed patiently on. There was no track that Alfredo could see, but Uncle Giorgio led them twisting up and up, always finding the easiest way, as if he had done this many times before. For a while they skirted an enormous silent chasm. Twice they passed near fissures from which rose wisps of yellowish reeking smoke. At last the sun dipped below the peak and for a short while they climbed in shadow, but soon the slope eased and they felt its force again. Briefly, the ground leveled, then dipped, and they were gazing into the crater of Etna.

Alfredo stared down. Before him lay a vast, ragged bowl, slopes of scarred and tumbled light gray rock and at the bottom a darker surface from which rose two cone-shaped mounds, like models of the mountain itself, each with a crater of its own. Dense smoke streamed steadily up from the farther one. The nearer one was still. To another boy, expecting to see a churning fiery surface threatening at any moment to boil up, fill the crater and flood down the mountainside in destroying torrents of molten lava, it would have been a disappointment. Alfredo stood enthralled.

Something was happening to him. He didn't understand it. He felt . . . bigger. Hugely bigger. Not bigger inside himself. He was still only a fleck of living matter on the enormous mountain. Bigger, somehow *outside* himself. Sometimes he used to play with Father's burning glass, fascinated by the way he could use its lens to focus the sunlight into an intense dot that in a few seconds could make a twist of dried grass leap into flame and shrivel into ash. Standing here on the summit of Etna, he had become that burning dot, filled with the pure fire of the sun. The mountain itself was the lens.

"You feel it?" said Uncle Giorgio.

"I could do anything!" whispered Alfredo.

"Yes," answered Uncle Giorgio just as quietly, drawing the syllable out to become a sigh of satisfaction, exulting in the knowledge of power. *He* knew what Alfredo was talking about.

Without thought Alfredo filled his lungs and started to sing.

"Let God arise, and let his enemies be scattered; let them also that hate him flee before Him.
"Like as the smoke vanisheth, so shalt thou drive them away; and like as wax melteth at the fire, so let the ungodly perish at the presence of God . . ."

Psalm 68 had always been his favorite. For him it was the fire psalm. Where better to sing it, rejoicing in the central fire? Immediately he was rapt, lost in the power of the music. The mountain itself seemed to be shuddering beneath

56

his feet. He was being battered to and fro. His head rang with a sudden stinging buffet, so that he lost his footing and fell, with all the breath and all the singing knocked out of him. Uncle Giorgio was dragging him to his feet, and the mountain really was shuddering beneath him.

"Quiet!" snapped Uncle Giorgio. "Stupid boy! See what you have done! Listen."

He was pointing down into the crater. A deep, throbbing rumble rose from below, but threaded through it Alfredo could faintly make out, right at the limits of his hearing, a high, fierce music. He recognized it at once, the voices of not one but a multitude of salamanders, and knew that they were answering his singing, rejoicing in their element.

The rumbling deepened and increased, and became a roar as the floor of the crater below him cracked apart in a great, suppurating red-and-black wound. A blast of roasting wind, reeking of sulphur, swept up the slope, and huge chunks of fiery matter were flung skyward like dead leaves caught in a wind eddy.

"Tell it no!" snapped Uncle Giorgio. "You began it. You must end it. I can only help you."

Alfredo looked at him, bewildered. He was staring out over the crater, erect and stiff, with his clenched fists held in front of his shoulders, waiting. Alfredo, not knowing what else to do, copied his stance. Uncle Giorgio glanced at him and nodded to him to begin.

How can you tell a mountain no?

The knowledge slid into his mind.

His earlier exhilaration returned, the outside power, the lens through which it poured, the burning dot—only the dot was now doubled, his own power overlaid with Uncle Giorgio's, one intense concentration of the pure power of the sun saying to the immense furnace below, "I am your Master. Be still."

And then it was over. He felt himself unfocussing, separating from the one-ness with his uncle, withdrawing . . . and he was standing, dizzy with effort, on the lip of the crater as the rocks rained down on the outer slopes and the fiery turmoil stilled and the roaring dwindled to a rumble and then to silence. The wind lifted the smoke aside until he could see the floor of the crater clearly. There was now a third small cone down there, with its own thin plume peacefully drifting away. Distantly in the stillness he could hear the singing of the salamanders, lulling the mountain to sleep.

Utterly dazed, half still exultant, half appalled, by the torrent of power that had rushed through him, he turned toward Uncle Giorgio, expecting a blast of anger at his rashness and folly. But Uncle Giorgio was smiling his thin smile and nodding with inward satisfaction. All he said was "Do not sing on the mountain again, not until you understand more of what you are doing."

"Isn't . . . isn't the mountain angry with us for stopping it?"

"It is always angry, but it knows its Master. Its Masters, I must say now. That is enough for today. Let us go home."

It was already drawing toward dusk as they made their way down the mountain. The whole of the Straits was laid out below them, with the fishing boats gathering toward the harbor and larger vessels sailing peacefully on. Alfredo barely noticed. He was still wrestling with what had happened up at the crater—not outside him, but inside. He had been changed. Such power! *I could do anything!*

But . . .

It had been wonderful, glorious, unimaginable even now, even in memory—memory wasn't big enough to contain it. . . .

But did he want it to happen again? And again, until he became in the end what the power made of him?

Like Uncle Giorgio, perhaps?

Could he even help that happening to him, now that he'd started?

He was appalled, terrified. But still deeply, deeply thrilled. Yes, though the actual experience continued to fade in his mind as they made their way down from the crater, it had not been a dream. By an exercise of pure power he had woken the mountain, and stilled it.

Now, suddenly the feelings returned. The mountain spoke in his mind. Not with its full thunder, but with a deep, rumbling whisper.

"Here."

Where? A little below him and to his left a small crag jutted from the slope. Beside it ran a hidden fault line in the underlying rocks, a place where the central fires rose close to the surface.

"Let me out," it seemed to be whispering to him. *"Let me burn."*

And he could have done it. If he had chosen, he could have reached them from here with his mind and woken the mountain again, and then stilled it.

Yes, and there had been another such place, much farther down, below the house, among the vineyards . . .

He halted for a moment, turned and gazed out to sea. Suppose . . .

Suppose its Master were absent or ill, could the mountain wake of its own accord and direct its power in a single beam that would set one of those boats blazing? Yes, it could.

And could Alfredo have held it back, as Uncle Giorgio said he had tried to do for the *Bonaventura,* and would have done if he hadn't been so close to dying?

No, not yet. He had the power, but not the skill. That was something he would need to learn.

How did he know these things? Nobody had told him, but he hadn't needed to work them out, or decide them. They were already there in his mind, certainties. They were part of something that had come to him at the summit, when he and Uncle Giorgio had been saying no to the mountain, focussed together, almost one person . . . a kind of leakage between them.

Down the slope Uncle Giorgio had halted and was looking inquiringly back to see why Alfredo had stopped.

Had anything leaked the other way, he wondered as he hurried on down. What secrets of his did Uncle Giorgio now know?

He was very grateful to Uncle Giorgio for all that he'd done for him, and almost sure that he wished him well, but what went on inside him—his thoughts and feelings, hopes, terrors, suspicions, guesses—that was private. If Uncle Giorgio knew anything about it . . .

He didn't like the idea at all.

It was almost dark before they reached the woods, but Uncle Giorgio took a lantern from the saddlebags, lit it with flint and tinder and led their way down the twisting track through the trees. It must have been midnight before they reached home, but the silent woman had supper waiting for them. Alfredo was more than half asleep by the time he climbed the stairs.

CHAPTER SIX

N EXT MORNING ALFREDO AGAIN WOKE LATE. His dreams had been full of fire, but all he could remember of them was a brief glimpse of two boys, far up the slopes of Etna, joyfully pelting each other with balls of fire.

The image haunted him as he dressed. Two brothers might play like that, if the power was in them. Father and Uncle Giorgio, for instance, before they quarrelled . . . There must have been a time . . . That's what the dream seemed to be telling him. . . . Or had they hated each other from the very first? He wanted to learn to love and trust Uncle Giorgio, who'd run such terrible risks, had very nearly died, for Alfredo's sake. His uncle wasn't the sort of person it was easy to love or trust, but he felt it was his duty. There was no way he could learn to unlove his own father, and just take Uncle Giorgio's side in the quarrel. But perhaps he could somehow heal the rift. Not between the brothers themselves any longer, now that one of them was dead, but perhaps somehow inside himself . . . If only he knew what had happened.

He ate his breakfast slowly, trying to think all this

through, and it was toward noon before he went to look for Uncle Giorgio. He found him, as yesterday, in his study, reading and making notes in the margin of his book. He looked up and arranged his features into a smile—with a bit more practice he would soon be quite good at that. He was certainly trying.

"You slept well, Alfredo?"

"Yes, thank you, Uncle. I dreamed about you, I think."

"A good dream, I hope?"

"Well, it felt happy while I was dreaming it. There were these two boys up on the mountain playing snowballs—there was snow one year at home and we all rushed out and snowballed each other—only these boys weren't using snow, they were doing it with fire . . . and I . . . I thought . . ."

He broke off as Uncle Giorgio rose abruptly from his chair and swung away to the window, where he stood staring out at the trees and tapping his fingernails on his wrist. When he spoke it was as if his throat had become suddenly sore again.

"You imagined that they might be your father and myself. No, Alfredo, we never did that. Nor could we have. Though we are Masters of the Mountain, given the chance its fire will consume our flesh as readily as it will any other man's. You think often of your father, Alfredo?"

"All the time. . . . I'm sorry, but . . . I know you didn't . . ."

"It is not to be wondered at. I do not blame you."

"Will you tell me why you . . . why you . . . not now. . . . I know you're busy, but . . ."

Uncle Giorgio turned from the window and came back to his chair and sat down.

"We disagreed about something of great importance to both of us," he said quietly. "Do you need to know more?"

"I . . . I loved him," said Alfredo. "He was . . . I don't know how to say it. . . . He was *everything*. But now . . . You've done a lot for me. You nearly killed yourself for me. I want to love you, too. But if you hated each other . . . You see . . . ?"

For a long while Uncle Giorgio didn't answer, but simply sat looking at him, once or twice shaking his head as if rejecting some thought.

"Too late . . . ," he muttered, and then, in a different, firmer tone, ". . . and too soon."

He turned back to his book, but after reading two or three lines he looked up with his thin, unreadable smile.

"You are an admirable child and have admirable sentiments," he said in his normal dry voice. "I have every confidence that the day will come when each of us loves the other as much as we love ourselves. But for the moment I am not ready to tell you what you think you want to know, and you are not ready to hear it. That time too will surely come, and then you will know as much about the matter as I do myself. But not this morning. This morning I will prepare and set you a task to do after luncheon. Meanwhile, go where you want, indoors or out. Nothing will harm you. Only if a door is locked, do not try to open it. This is your home now, and you must learn its ways, as I and your father did when we were boys."

For a while, as he set off to explore, Alfredo seemed to

be almost back in his dream. Surely the house had something to tell him of those vanished years. The upper floor was arranged on the same plan as the lower one. A wide corridor stretched from end to end of the house, with shorter corridors at either end running back toward the mountain. Only two of these upstairs rooms appeared to be used, his own and Uncle Giorgio's. This wasn't one of the grander ones looking out east over the Straits, but lay round at the northwest corner of the house, immediately above the study, with one window facing the mountain and another the trees. A bleak, bare room with a shabby carpet; a narrow, unornamented bed; two chairs; a huge, dark wardrobe and a plain table covered with books. A smaller table beside the bed held a lamp and several medicine bottles. On another small table was a birdcage occupied by a starling, smaller than the one in the study, and with stronger mottling on its breast feathers. It eyed Alfredo, standing in the door. It didn't speak, but squawked as he left the room. There were no pictures, of saints or anything else. Not even a crucifix on the wall.

All the other doors on the upper floor opened onto shuttered rooms, about twenty of them in all, some with huge beds whose moth-eaten hangings glinted with gold thread, others completely unfurnished. All smelled of mice, and old mortar crumbling into dust from summer after roasting summer, but as he opened each door Alfredo could almost sense the movements of two faint figures just vanished through the connecting door into the room beyond.

The ground floor was more interesting. Four huge rooms faced the sea, two on either side of the central hallway. Bars of sunlight slanted through the cracks of their shutters. The northernmost one was a library, with shelves of great dark books reaching toward the ceiling. The furniture was swathed in dust sheets. Curious, Alfredo lifted the corner of a sheet covering a slab almost as large as the high altar in the cathedral and found an ornately carved desk. There was a litter of bird skeletons and feathers under its central tunnel, where a cat or something must have laired. It no longer smelled of rot, so that must have been years ago.

Next to the library was a reception room twice the size, with its furniture also sheeted, and on the other side of the hallway an equally enormous dining room. The two shadowy presences seemed just to have slipped through its farther doors. Unconsciously Alfredo quickened his pace as he walked along beside the table, counting the sheeted chairs as he passed. Twenty-four on either side, and two at each end. Fifty. He wondered when fifty ladies and gentlemen had last dined here. Oh, for a whisper of their talk, some whiff of that ancient feasting!

Last, in the southeast corner of the house, was a music room. There were three curving rows of chairs where the same ladies and gentlemen might have sat and sipped their coffee and gossiped in whispers as they half-listened to the tinklings of the two sheeted harpsichords, the thump of the sheeted drums, the whining of the fiddles and tweeting of the flutes and recorders that hung in cases between the windows. Alfredo took a treble recorder from a rack, breathed into it and fingered the stops. The scale came as sweet and true as if it had last played yesterday. But when he lifted the sheet from the front of one of the harpsichords and tried the keyboard, he got nothing but thumps and creaks.

Coming so soon after the recorder's sweetness, the dismal sounds spoke to him.

No, they seemed to be saying. *Those elegant evenings are gone, long gone. They won't come back.*

He closed the lid and pulled the sheet back over it, and as he left the music room he realized that the two ghosts he had been following had also gone.

The rooms on the other side of the central corridor were smaller. One still seemed to be some kind of estate office, two others were storerooms, the rest were shuttered and sheeted. He could not guess what they'd once been used for. Indeed most of the huge house no longer had any purpose that he could see or feel. How could this be his—anybody's—home? How could he spend his days—his life—in this emptiness? Alone with a dumb woman and an apparent idiot. And Uncle Giorgio.

Uncle Giorgio. Something had happened in the study that morning. For a few moments—for a few words only— *"Too late . . . and too soon"*—there had seemed to be a different Uncle Giorgio. Different in what way? In . . . in *thereness.* This was something Alfredo hadn't realized about Uncle Giorgio before. Normally, even when you were with him, he was somehow utterly alone. Only sometimes, faintly—when Alfredo had been singing to him, or when he'd just drunk the salamander's tears and healed his throat—had he been *there* in the way he'd been there with Alfredo in the study for those few moments. But then, immediately afterward, he'd been alone again, and talking out of that loneliness in words that perhaps meant one thing on Alfredo's side of the barrier and something quite different on his own. Perhaps that's what he'd been smiling about—those different meanings. They'd amused him.

"The day will come when each of us loves the other as much as we love ourselves."

But you didn't love other people like that. You loved them from the *outside*. Perhaps Uncle Giorgio didn't know very much about love. No, it wasn't going to be easy. But who else was there?

He worked his way back through these lesser rooms to the corridor leading to Uncle Giorgio's study. Reluctant to go farther, and desperate for human company, company of any kind, he turned back and along the similar corridor at the southern end of the house. The first room here was the one they ate in, and beyond that, presumably, the kitchens—at least the silent woman brought their meals from that direction. Yes, because the third door he came to was open, and through it he could see her standing in front of a grim old iron stove. At the sound of his footstep she turned, frowning.

"May I come in?" he said.

She nodded and turned back to the stove. By her movement and attitude he guessed that the frown had not been for him, and as soon as he was in the room he knew what the trouble was. The chimney was drawing well enough, but the fire itself was out of balance—"unhappy," Father would have said. He crossed the floor and knelt beside the woman. As he opened the fire door she gave a warning hiss.

"It's all right," he said. "I know about ovens. My father's a baker. Was."

One sniff of the curious bitter reek of the smoke told him what the problem was. Elder is a mean wood, and always has been. No careful baker will have it in his stack, or anywhere near. There was a story that a smith once refused to shoe a pilgrim's ass for charity, and St. Martin cursed the man, saying that the timber from the trees round his smithy would never again draw true. They were elders, of course. Even Father, who had little time for saint lore, almost believed the tale. The log would reek the kitchen out if he tried to remove it now, so he rose and rummaged though the timber stack behind the stove, choosing two billets of well-dried ash, always an easy-tempered wood, and better yet, a stout piece of old olive that would burn with a steady, golden heat right to its last embers. He eased them in round the elder and closed the door. Before he had finished adjusting the dampers he could feel the fire steadying to its work. A couple minutes later the woman sensed it too, for she turned to him, smiling, and bowed her head in thanks.

"My pleasure," said Alfredo. He sorted through the stack, picking out the elder logs. When he'd found them all he showed one to the woman.

"Bad wood," he said. "Where shall I put them?"

She pointed to a door, and he carried them out and found himself in a courtyard between the two wings, with the main house to his right, and to his left a range of stables and storage sheds. Behind these he found the log piles, so he stacked the pieces of elder neatly to one side and carried an armful of better wood back to the kitchen to replace them. The woman smiled her thanks once more as he returned, and he settled onto one of the benches by the kitchen table. The company of the woman, however silent, was better than the emptiness of the rest of the house, and the company of a working fire almost as good.

After a while the strange young man came in from the garden, saw Alfredo and turned to run, but the woman clucked at him and he came creeping on in and sat at the end of the other bench, as far as he could get from Alfredo. The woman ladled food from a pot and put it in front of him, with a hunk of coarse bread. He grasped her hand— for reassurance about this stranger, Alfredo guessed—and she rumpled his hair affectionately. The man ate his meal with a spoon, sitting sideways at the table, hunching protectively over his bowl and glancing at Alfredo every mouthful, like a dog fearful that its food is about to be snatched away by a bigger dog. As soon as he'd eaten he crept out.

A

Uncle Giorgio brought a book to luncheon to be alone with, but after a while he half-closed it, keeping his finger in the page, and glanced inquiringly at Alfredo. Alfredo took his chance.

"The woman—I don't think she can talk—and the man who was working in the garden when we came . . . ?"

"What of them?"

"Who are they? I mean, I don't even know their names. . . ."

"Her name is Annetta and his Toni. He is her son. She was born dumb, but otherwise healthy. He in his turn was born with his mind deformed. The true cause was a defect in the father's seed, but the people of this island are very ignorant. Her family believed him to be a child of some demon and would have killed them both. I took them in and sheltered them, and in return they work for me."

Alfredo had been mopping up oil from his plate with a corner of bread. He stopped for a moment, and then managed to carry on, still staring at what he was doing as if it had been all that mattered to him, but inwardly stiff with shock. It wasn't the words, it was the tone his uncle had used, as if everything to do with the story disgusted him, and his own part in it had been a repellent duty. Father might have helped the woman in just the same way, and spoken of what he'd done in much those words, but oh, how different in feeling! No warmth of love and pity for the woman and her child, no heat of anger at the stupidity and superstition of the people, but cold contempt for both her and them, and most of all, or so it sounded, for the father and the defect in his seed.

He looked up. Uncle Giorgio had re-opened his book but was still looking at him. He groped for a change of subject.

"You wanted me to do something this afternoon."

His uncle breathed slowly out through his nostrils, as if clearing Annetta and her son from his mind, and answered in a more normal voice.

"Go to your room and learn this by heart," he said, drawing a folded piece of paper from his pocket. "Both the words and the music. You will not find it easy, as the words are Old Persian, but I have written them out as they are pronounced. The music is from the same country, and unlike either what you sang in the cathedral or the songs you seem to have picked up in the streets. I have used plainsong notation, as being the least unlike the Persian. Do your best. We have not many days before you need to be both word perfect and note perfect. Annetta will come for you when I am ready."

"Will you tell me what the words mean, Uncle Giorgio? It's easier like that. That's why I was keen to learn Latin. Some of the other boys didn't—"

"They would remain meaningless even if I told you. They are, in fact, in the sacred language of the Old Persian priests, who worshipped the sun. They used the chant to invoke certain powers that emanate from the sun. The ignorant might call them demons, but they are in fact Angels of Fire, such as were seen walking with Shadrach, Meshach and Abednego in the furnace of King Nebuchadnezzar."

Alfredo studied the paper as he made his way up to his room. It seemed to have been freshly written, presumably by Uncle Giorgio that very morning. The music certainly looked strange, though the choir used to sing plainsong on Fridays in Lent, and some other fast days. Some of the longer notes were marked in a way he didn't understand. The words were even stranger, full of letters that couldn't possibly go together despite what Uncle Giorgio said— *zch, gj, qb*—things like that. How could he learn this stuff if he couldn't even say it?

He settled in the window, looking east across the strait.

The sun had passed behind the house, but still lit the long slope below him, and the baked earth poured its warmth back into the slow wind that swept up from the sea. Other boys might have found its heat too much to bear, but for Alfredo it was strength, life, hope. He felt he was actually in the presence of those Angels of Fire of whom Uncle Giorgio had spoken, invisible but there, riding the hot wind. If the chant was for them, surely he could learn to sing it.

A memory sidled into his mind. The harbor at home. Alfredo minding the donkey while Father inspected flour, dipping into the sack, running the fine, yellowish powder through his fingers, raising a palmful to his nose to sniff. The flour was of an expensive Moroccan wheat. The ship was from Tangier, very different from the French and Spanish vessels that mostly traded into this port, lower in the water and with a vast, striped sail that hung furled in sagging bundles from one long spar. There was a young man sitting cross-legged in the bow, pattering on a drum in his lap while he sang in a high nasal wail, rapid repetitive notes tailing away into longer ones sung with a curious gargling tremolo. Alfredo didn't think Morocco was any-where near Persia, and the sailor's song wouldn't have fit-ted the notes he'd been staring at, but he could see at once that if he'd needed to write that song down this was how he'd have tried to do it. It was the same kind of music.

Tentatively he tried it out, *la-la-la*, feeling foolish, knowing he was nowhere near the music he was supposed to be singing, or anyone would want to listen to, let alone anything he could believe he could conjure the Angels of

Fire with. When the choir had been learning something new, singing it *la-la-la,* the music had never seemed to come alive for him till they'd started to fit the words in. Even these impossible words might be better than *la-la-las.* Without any hope at all he gave it a go.

The notes slid smoothly out of his throat and his mouth shaped them into something like the mysterious syllables. And in a moment they were there, the Angels of Fire, visible presences, soaring like hawks in the steadily rising air. Their bodies were great embers, rippling with inner heat. They had the faces of lions, maned around with flame, and their wings were plumed with flame. Their glances were the lightning that sparks the drought-parched hills ablaze.

Terrified, remembering what had almost happened when he had sung the fire psalm on the crater of Etna, Alfredo closed his lips and clamped both hands across them. Instantly the breeze was once again empty air. Shuddering despite the heat, he retreated into the room. What had he done? Was it too late to undo it? Uncle Giorgio would know, but . . . did he dare face that cold anger, and tell him? Yes, he decided, he must.

When he reached the study he had to force his hand to scratch at the door. Uncle Giorgio called, and he pushed it open. It was just as bad as he'd feared.

"What is this? I said I would send for you."

"Please, Uncle . . . I may have . . . I saw them . . . the Angels of Fire . . . when I sang the words . . ."

The anger vanished, leaving only the coldness, the aloneness.

"You have learned the chant already?"

"Only the first line. It was there. In my mouth. In my head. I don't know what the words mean, but the music . . . I once heard this sailor . . . the ship was from Tangier . . ."

Uncle Giorgio cut him short with a gesture.

"Some there have the Knowledge," he said, "though theirs is of the sea. Tell me what you did and what you saw."

"I was sitting at my window trying to learn the music, but I couldn't, not without the words, though I wasn't sure I could even say them. But when I tried I could, and then I saw the Angels. They were gliding on the wind. Like burning birds. I stopped as soon as I saw them. I remembered . . ."

"I had not thought the chant would be effective without my presence. Never mind. Sing what you have learned so far. You may read it if you wish. Is there anything you wish to ask me first?"

"Yes, please. How do I say this—you've written it g, h, z—and this . . . ?"

"Come here. Give me the paper."

With Alfredo looking over his shoulder, Uncle Giorgio read the whole chant slowly through while Alfredo silently mouthed the words behind him.

He handed the paper back and Alfredo sang the first line, hesitantly, stumbling so that he barely held the chant. Mouth and throat had forgotten most of what they'd seemed to know up at his window. The line was repeated and he managed better second time through. Uncle Giorgio seemed to be only half listening. His face was set, his eyes half closed, and once or twice he whispered a few words beneath his breath. As the last long note faded Alfredo glanced out the window, half expecting to see the Angels of Fire sweeping past on the wind, but nothing stirred except the leaves of the trees, not one burning feather or flake of flame.

"Yes," said Uncle Giorgio slowly, "you have the idea. Indeed, you appear to have come to me formed and ready for your destiny."

A pause, and then, with bitter force, "In you, at least, the blood runs true."

Alfredo, still with half his mind on the difficult music and half on the Angels of Fire, was jolted into attention. His uncle was staring at him with the same intent strange gaze as when they'd been eating their meal on the mountainside. The sudden anger of the last few words startled him into awareness. Though the anger didn't seem to be directed at him, it was as if a horrible dark pit had opened suddenly at his feet.

"One! Two! Three! Four!" shrieked the starling, breaking the spell.

Uncle Giorgio picked up his book and said, "Learn what you can of the rest without trying to sing it, and we will then choose times when you can practice in my presence, so that I can control matters as you cannot—not yet. Wait. You had best not sing anything at all unless I am there. This place is full of ancient powers that you may inadvertently awaken. Now you may go."

CHAPTER SEVEN

Lfredo left, even more bewildered than he'd been when he'd come. He stopped at the foot of the stairs, unable to face the loneliness of his room. Strange that he'd crept down here straightforwardly scared of Uncle Giorgio's anger, and though Uncle Giorgio hadn't been angry after all—had merely accepted what had happened as an unlucky accident—Alfredo felt he would have preferred the anger to what had in fact happened. Anger at least would have been contact of a sort, a kind of nearness, however uncomfortable. But after those first few moments, even when Alfredo had been standing directly behind his shoulder, learning how to pronounce the words of the chant, Uncle Giorgio had seemed unreachable distances away, barricaded in the fortress of his aloneness.

Yes, he had sounded pleased by how well Alfredo had got on with learning the chant, but pleased in the wrong way, not pleased *with* Alfredo, his nephew, another human being like himself, but pleased *about* what had happened, in the way a farmer might be pleased about rain on his vines.

And what did he mean about Alfredo's destiny? To become Master of the Mountain one day? That was the obvious meaning. But Uncle Giorgio didn't talk in obvious meanings. Anyway, Alfredo didn't think he wanted a destiny. A destiny wasn't anything you had any control over, any choice about. It was something that happened to you, whether you liked it or not. Something Uncle Giorgio wanted to happen. That was what he'd been pleased about.

And that sudden bitter outburst, *"At least in you the blood runs true!"* So there was someone else, someone in whom it didn't . . . and who wasn't going to have a destiny because of that? Poor brave brother Giorgio, who'd rushed into the blazing bakehouse to try to save his parents? Uncle Giorgio hadn't been interested in his namesake, though he'd come to his christening. But he hadn't come to his name-day, or sent him a present, and he'd pushed straight past him at Alfredo's christening. So he must have seen that first time that Giorgio didn't have what he was looking for, just as he'd seen that Alfredo did.

But what had Giorgio ever done to deserve such anger? No, not Giorgio. But the someone must have been older than him, or Uncle Giorgio wouldn't have needed to come at all.

There were certainly secrets. How could there not be? Uncle Giorgio was a sorcerer. Alfredo had felt his power as they had stood on the rim of Etna's crater and quieted the mountain's seething fires. But he had felt his own powers waken there as he'd joined the task. Did that mean that he, too, was a sorcerer? Was sorcery what ran in his blood? Sorcery was a mortal sin because it meant consorting with demons. Were the Angels of Fire, so strong and beautiful, demons? And the salamander, who had wept with Alfredo over the loss of all he loved?

Too many questions. All he could do was take them one by one, and find out what happened next. So the first thing to do was to learn the chant. How, if he wasn't allowed to sing it?

A thought came to him, and instead of climbing the stairs he went on along the corridor into the music room and took the treble recorder from its rack. If he couldn't sing the music, perhaps he could play it, fix it in his head that way, silently fitting the words to the notes as he went along. Not in here, though. It was too close to Uncle Giorgio's uncomfortable presence. He made his way out through the empty kitchen, through the blazing heat of the yard and explored southward. Long ago somebody must have terraced and planted this part of the slope to make a formal garden overlooking the magnificent view across the Straits. Now it was overgrown, mostly with the same scrub that covered the uncultivated bits of hillside, mixed in with huge old garden roses, unpruned for years, and the somber rusty-looking columns of ancient cypresses rising in regular rows above the tangle. He followed a path that still seemed used and came to a circular sunken area surrounded by a stone balustrade, with a dry pond and fountain at the center, and statues of old Romans here and there.

This seemed just what he wanted. There was even a stone bench, at this hour in the long shadow of a cypress on the terrace above. He settled there, and instead of starting straight in on the chant decided to get his hands used to the fingering of the recorder with tunes he already knew. The Precentor at the cathedral had encouraged the boys to learn a musical instrument. Some became highly skilled, but Alfredo had been far more interested in singing and had never progressed beyond the recorder. Still, he could play, and now found it comforting in a melancholy kind of way to fill the silence of this forgotten southern garden with the familiar songs of home.

How shall we sing the Lord's song in a strange land?

He thought of the salamander, of their shared grief and loss, and almost wept again as he played. It was some while before he realized he was being watched.

He felt the watcher's presence before he turned. All he saw was a quick furtive movement at the top of the steps, but he guessed at once who the watcher, now crouching behind the balustrade, must be. Still with his eyes on the steps he put the recorder to his lips and played on. Slowly Toni emerged and crept down the steps, but stopped on the last one. For a while he just stood there, staring, then lifted his hands in a beseeching gesture such as small children use, reaching longing hands toward some bright new toy, but very strange in a full-grown man. Alfredo stopped playing and held out the recorder, offering it to Toni. Toni inched forward, but couldn't force his feet to carry him more than halfway to the bench, so Alfredo put the recorder down, rose and walked off round the empty pool. As soon as he was safely the other side of it Toni darted forward, snatched up the recorder, put it to his lips and blew.

Of course no sound came. Toni frowned and looked across at Alfredo. Alfredo raised an imaginary recorder to his mouth, placing his fingertips carefully to the invisible stops, and blew gently. Toni studied the recorder and put it to his lips again. His fingers seemed to find their way onto the stops of their own accord. He blew, fluttering them up and down. Notes of a sort emerged. Quite deliberately he started to experiment, discovering one by one what the individual finger movements achieved. Then, astoundingly, he arranged them into a scale. And then, even more astonishingly, he was playing, note perfect, the tune Alfredo had been playing twenty minutes before. When he reached the end he started again, ornamenting the simple tune with pleasing variations. By now he had forgotten to be afraid. He was rapt, lost in the music. Alfredo felt a great surge of sympathy and fellowship. He had known what this was like, when he himself had been caught up, transported, as he and the whole choir used to pour their souls into a *Te Deum* or *Magnificat* in the cathedral, and nothing else existed but themselves and the music.

Where had it come from? he wondered. Who had taught Toni the scales?

Nobody. It must be something to do with this place, something to do with the salamanders.

Toni finished the tune and lowered the recorder. He stared around with a dazed look in his eyes. Alfredo watched him come back to the bitter understanding of who and where and what he was. His face crumpled. He flung the recorder on the ground and rushed whimpering up the steps and out of sight.

Alfredo picked up the recorder, climbed the steps and gazed around, half expecting some fresh eruption of fire magic to have been awakened by their music, but all he saw was the long slope below him and the heat-hazed view across the Straits, all he heard was the endless whine of cicadas reinforcing the stillness of a late-summer afternoon.

He made his way back to the house by the same route he'd come. Annetta was in the kitchen, paring vegetables. Toni would be very upset, he guessed, so it was only fair to tell her why. She too was clearly disturbed, but managed to make him see that she wasn't angry with him.

"Is it bad for him?" he asked. "He looked so happy while he was playing, but if you want me to hide the recorder . . ."

She shook her head, pointed to the wall opposite the stove and put her finger to her lips. He understood at once. She was pointing at Uncle Giorgio's study in the opposite wing of the house. *Don't tell Giorgio.*

He nodded and repeated her gesture.

He put the recorder back in its rack and went up to his room. As he climbed the stairs he realized that he had found the exchange comforting. It meant several things: chiefly that he now didn't need to make up his mind whether to tell Uncle Giorgio what had happened; but also that Uncle Giorgio's powers were limited—he wasn't instantly aware of everything that happened in and around his house, even when it was somehow involved with magic, as Toni's almost magical discovery of his gift for music must have been; and thirdly that Annetta herself wasn't Uncle Giorgio's devoted slave but an intelligent and independent woman who might even accept Alfredo as a friend. And perhaps he could make friends with Toni, too.

It would be a strange friendship, lived in music. But that was a good enough place to live.

Uncle Giorgio brought a book to supper and read while he ate, so at first it was a silent meal. After a while he seemed to notice the fact and laid his book aside.

"I apologize," he said. "I am used to reading over my meals. Perhaps you should do the same, at least until we have come to some arrangement for your education. There are Latin histories on the upper shelves of column D—Livius should be within your grasp—and there are dictionaries below and to their left. I fear that there is not much in the house to amuse a child. You must see what you can find."

"Oh, thank you," said Alfredo. "There's a little recorder in the music room. Is it all right if I play that?"

"Why not?"

"I thought it might be a way of learning the chant without actually singing it."

"Ah . . . Yes, if it helps. But if anything happens stop at once and come and tell me," said Uncle Giorgio, and returned to his book.

So after supper Alfredo explored the library, using a cunning folding ladder to climb to the top shelves. He found the Livius history and a battered old Latin dictionary small enough to carry around, and then hunted for something more amusing. Most of the books were too large to handle comfortably, and in strange heavy lettering, difficult to read, or in languages he didn't know. There were others whose alphabet wasn't the one used for Latin and Italian. Most of these he recognized as Greek, but some were even stranger, Arabic or Turkish, he guessed, or Persian, like the words of the chant. He didn't find anything about salamanders or other kinds of fire magic, nor a history of the di Salas or anything useful about the mountain, though there was some stuff about it in a huge Geography of Sicily, as big as a small tabletop. He guessed that all the magic books—anything with secrets in it—would be in Uncle Giorgio's study. He took the ones he'd chosen, fetched the recorder upstairs.

For a while he sat in the window, doggedly working through stories about ancient kings. Then, leafing through the dictionary in search of a word, he found a folded sheet of paper somebody must have been using as a bookmark. Unfolded, it turned out to be a series of jottings—notes, he guessed, on some book the writer had been reading, using the dictionary to help him. The handwriting was old-fashioned and hard to decipher, but a word caught his eye. *Salamandri.* The word before that looked like *lacrimae.* *Lacrimae salamandri.* The tears of the salamander. Excited now, he forgot about the history and until it became too dark to read he wrestled with the notes. It wasn't Uncle Giorgio's writing—nobody alive now, but someone long ago. There were scrawls he couldn't read at all. Even in the better-written bits there mostly weren't enough words he could make out to get any sense out of the Latin. By the time it got too dark to read he'd got as far as *the tears of the salamander . . . against all ills of the flesh,* and from what Uncle Giorgio had said he knew that the missing word had to mean *sovereign,* though it didn't seem to be in the dictionary. Lower down there was something about *one who has knowledge* and *Angels of Fire, Greater or Lesser.* He gave up as it was getting too dark to read, and played the recorder and watched the stars rise one by one over Italy.

CHAPTER EIGHT

NEXT MORNING HE WAS WOKEN BY A SCRATCHing at the door, and by the time his eyes were properly open Annetta was in the room, laying out clothes on his bed and making signs for him to get up and dress. The clothes were stiff and smelled of long storage, and were far grander than he was used to, dark breeches, a ruffled shirt, a brown velvet jacket with brass buttons and black braid trimmings, and buckled shoes, but they fitted well enough. Perhaps Uncle Giorgio had worn them when he was a boy, or perhaps Father. Downstairs he found Uncle Giorgio already halfway through his breakfast. He was dressed in the grand clothes in which Alfredo had first seen him, but without the sword.

"You must eat quickly," he said. "It is Sunday, and we go to Mass."

They walked together down the mountain, with Annetta and Toni following well behind and leading two of the mules. The sound of church bells was already floating up the town before they reached the vineyards, and the service was just beginning by the time they were at the church. A verger met them at a side door, bowing to Uncle Giorgio, and cleared a way for them through the crowded transept up into the choir, where he showed them into two elaborately carved stalls that faced east toward the high altar. Alfredo noticed the coat of arms above his seat. The shield had a salamander on it. The missal and psaltery on the shelf in front of him had the same coat stamped onto their bindings. Most of the stalls on the other side of the church were occupied, but the ones immediately to the right of where he sat were empty. The shields above their seats were carved with the head of a horse.

Uncle Giorgio knelt and prayed. Alfredo did the same, grieving for his own lost world, the bakehouse and the cathedral and the people he'd loved. The choir were singing, or attempting to sing, music he knew well. The trebles were thin and squeaky, and both tenors erratic on their top notes. Without thought he improvised a descant, almost under his breath, too quietly for anyone else to hear, but Uncle Giorgio immediately tapped him on the shoulder and shook his head, frowning.

He fell silent. His mind wandered. It was a while before he became aware of a difference. A difference from what? From . . . yes, from the world outside. The mountain. Wherever he'd been on the island, and from far out to sea, waking or sleeping, the mountain had been simply *there*, a vast presence, a pressure. Not here, in this church. For all he could feel of it, nothing might lie outside these walls but endless level plain. For the moment he was free of it. Free. It was almost as though the force of gravity no longer bound him to the earth and he could fly, as he sometimes could in dreams. He glanced at Uncle Giorgio, wondering if he felt the same, but as usual his face told nothing.

As the choir began to process down the aisle at the end of the service Uncle Giorgio left his stall, signed to Alfredo to do the same and joined the procession behind the priest. No one else did so. The procession filed into the vestry, but the priest stopped at the door, turned and bowed to Uncle Giorgio, who acknowledged the greeting with a nod.

"I must introduce you to my nephew and heir, Father Hippolyto," he said. "This is Alfredo di Sala. His parents died recently in a tragic accident, and he has come to live with me."

The priest, a tall but sagging man with heavy, pasty jowls, seemed to wince with surprise. His hand trembled as he took Alfredo's and his voice fluttered as he answered.

"I am honored indeed," he said. "The di Salas have long been our generous patrons, and I pray that they may long continue."

"I hope so too," said Alfredo politely.

"We will see you again next Sunday, I trust," said the priest, clearly trusting nothing of the sort.

"Of course," said Uncle Giorgio, and turned away with a faint smile on his lips, as though he was enjoying the priest's discomfort. Alfredo followed, wondering whether the priest was ill, that he trembled so, or only in awe of the grand gentleman, or actually afraid.

They came out of the chill of the church into the blaze of a southern noon, but Alfredo barely noticed the change, because in the same moment the mountain had returned and its pressure closed around him.

He stopped dead in his tracks. Uncle Giorgio looked down at him.

"You will need to get used to it," he said.

"It's all right. It was just a surprise. I think I *am* getting used to it. But it was nice being out of it for a bit."

"Not merely nice, necessary. I miss very few Sundays. As Father Hippolyto implied, I am an excellent son of the Church."

"I could sing in there, couldn't I, without . . . er . . . anything happening?"

"You are no longer a chorister, Alfredo," said Uncle Giorgio severely. "You are a gentleman, and must learn to act as such."

He sounded and looked entirely serious, but then his lips twitched briefly. It was so unexpected that Alfredo answered with a smile. Uncle Giorgio, straight-faced again, accepted the smile with a nod and walked on.

Alfredo followed, feeling that this once, for the moment, they understood each other. Whatever they might be on the mountain, down here in the town the di Salas were a family of proud and ancient lineage. It was genuinely and unarguably so, but at the same time it was a kind of act, because they weren't only that. They were also sorcerers of a power that no lineage could match.

It was as if in that shared understanding Alfredo had been allowed on the other side of a barrier, into Uncle Giorgio's aloneness, into a place where words meant something different from what they seemed to mean, and he understood those meanings. Then, in a few paces, the moment was over. It was Alfredo himself who ended it, shrinking back out of that aloneness, as if knowing by instinct that he would never be able to breathe its pure and joyless air.

Annetta and Toni were waiting with the mules by a mounting block at the side door, Toni cringing down between the animals out of sight from all the people and Annetta gripping his arm so that he shouldn't actually turn and run. Alfredo climbed clumsily onto the second mule, which without any signal from its rider at once set off after Uncle Giorgio's.

The square in front of the church was thronged, but nobody greeted Uncle Giorgio as he led the way across it. If anything, people seemed deliberately to be looking the other way and yet somehow to move out of his path. Alfredo saw a group dressed like gentry gossiping on the steps of the church, while a carriage and an open landau, each with a coat of arms on its door, waited below. One of the shields was painted with the head of a horse. The empty stalls next to his must belong to these people. Why hadn't they been using them? Were even they so afraid of Uncle Giorgio that they didn't want to worship beside him? Did everybody down here know what he was on the mountain, and were they all afraid of him? Did they all hate him in their hearts? Was that why no one would look at him?

Was that what happened when you became Master of the Mountain? Would it be the same with Alfredo himself one day, Sunday after Sunday coming down to face that fear and hate and pretending to worship, because the church was necessary to him, as it had been to his ancestors through the long generations? Had they too been hated and feared, as Uncle Giorgio was now? And Alfredo, too, when his turn came?

No, absolutely not, he decided. He would not join Uncle Giorgio in his aloneness. He would not pay that price of fear and hatred. If those were things the mountain demanded, it would have to find itself a different Master.

These feelings deepened and hardened as the mules plodded steadily up between the vineyards. He was conscious of Annetta following on foot, but falling farther and farther behind. Why should he be allowed to ride and Annetta have to walk? She was older than he was, and worked all day long while he did almost nothing to help. It wasn't right, any more than it had been right that Uncle Giorgio should have talked about her and Toni the way he had when he'd told Alfredo their story. Two harmless and unlucky people—but if Uncle Giorgio both used and despised them in the way he seemed to, how could Alfredo—how could *anybody*—learn to love and trust him?

Not that these thoughts came to him in a steady, reasoned flow. They were more a muddle of slowly changing feelings that shaped themselves into glimpses of thought that then hardened into ideas. And now something else, something from outside himself, worked its way into the confusion. When he and Uncle Giorgio had first climbed this path everything had been swamped by the overwhelming presence of the mountain, and the huge energies surging inside it. Then, two days ago, when they had climbed to the crater, he had begun to perceive some of its inner shape, the movements of its molten currents, the places of power where they came closer to the surface, and where their energies could be summoned and directed by someone who had the power and knowledge—Uncle Giorgio now, Alfredo himself, perhaps, later.

It was one of these places, not on the path itself, but up the slope to their left, that now broke into his chain of thought. He looked around and saw that this was where he had waited on that first afternoon while Uncle Giorgio had climbed up between the vines. This was the point from which he had watched the *Bonaventura* burst inexplicably into flame.

Uncle Giorgio rode past without pausing. Alfredo was following with no more than an inward shudder when the memory worked its way into his vague doubts and discomforts to produce a definite question. A question with two possible answers.

According to Uncle Giorgio, the mountain had been furious with the *Bonaventura* and his friends for returning its Master to it, and so had destroyed them. If so, then why at that particular moment, when the Master was closest to a place of power, and had most hope of preventing the destruction? Was the mountain just a brainless embodied anger, which had burst out at that moment, regardless of where its Master happened to be?

Or had Uncle Giorgio caused the mountain to do it, choosing this place because, despite his illness, here he still had the power? If so, why? Surely not just out of revenge on the captain for speaking to him as he had. No, it would bc because he was determined to remove any witnesses of their journey. Nobody must know that this was where he had brought his nephew. That was how much Alfredo mattered to him, that he would kill four innocent men to preserve his secret. Not for Alfredo's sake, but for his own.

Either was possible. Alfredo's mind wavered to and fro. He reached the house with his determination to trust Uncle Giorgio badly shaken, and only one decision made. He must talk to the salamander as soon as he got the chance.

ꟼ

Luck was with him for once. Annetta and Toni were still way down the mountain, but she had left food in covered dishes for them. They had both brought books to the table, and Uncle Giorgio helped himself, sat down and at once started to read, but as soon as Alfredo was seated he closed his book and pushed it aside.

"You ask remarkably few questions," he said. "Have you no more?"

"Oh, yes, but . . . I didn't want to bother you, but . . . Well, I was wondering about the salamanders. Somebody once told me that if you ask them something they will tell you the truth. Is that right?"

"Yes and no. The truth is in their music. For us, truth exists almost entirely in words. The salamanders do not use words. How can they speak our truth? I have heard you sing, Alfredo. You have an excellent voice and a good understanding, but you sing with the human emotions that are in the words, and this, as it were, contaminates the music. Even our unsung music may be contaminated by the human emotions of the player. But for the salamanders, their truth is in the notes, not in the manner in which the notes are sung. So if you would converse with the salamanders you must train yourself to sing without any emotion that can be put into words. When I converse with my salamander I normally use the fiddle. Before you came I used to sing to it only when I needed my hands to collect its tears. You must learn to treat your voice purely as a musical instrument, like my fiddle. Otherwise the truth that the salamander tells you will be contaminated with apparent meanings, which are in fact no more than echoes of your own hopes and fears. I have so far allowed you to sing to the salamander in that fashion because your singing achieved what was necessary, but before you can attain true understanding of the mountain, and of the task before you, you must train yourself to do as I say. Do you understand?"

"I think so. The organist in the cathedral used to have arguments with the Precentor about it, but the Prince-Cardinal agreed with the Precentor, so that's what I'm used to—singing as if I meant it, I mean."

"Whereas I agree with the organist, so you must do your best to unlearn what you have been taught."

"Last time I sang to the salamander I thought it showed me what it used to be like, living inside the mountain."

"Of course. But in fact it showed you no more than your own imaginings. When I was a boy I used to have such imaginings, but I trained myself to reject them. When we have eaten you can sing to the salamander again, and practice as you do so."

"*Super flumina?* Psalm One Thirty-seven?"

"What you sing is irrelevant, provided it is expressive of sadness."

"I felt very sad today when we were coming back up the hill. I was thinking about the sailors on the *Bonaventura*, and me singing the bit about the storm for them from Psalm One Hundred and Seven. It was only last Sunday, and now they're dead. Would that be all right?"

"Why that? It is a psalm of praise, I think. The music is not in itself sad."

"I could sing a requiem first."

"That would be better. And then you may sing the psalm if you wish."

Uncle Giorgio spoke flatly, as if he'd forgotten all about the *Bonaventura*. He was opening his book when he seemed to realize what they'd been talking about, and looked up again.

"I am truly sorry about what happened to our friends on the ship," he said. "But we must start to put all that behind us. We have great work to do, Alfredo, you and I."

He returned to his book and read for the rest of the meal.

There was now a curved sheet of metal supported on a wooden framework a little distance back from the furnace. Uncle Giorgio stationed Alfredo behind it.

"Lead," he explained. "It will shield your body from the harmful emanations of the furnace. Your head I can do nothing about until I have more lead, but it should not matter for the moment. It is frequent and prolonged exposure to the emanations that is dangerous. Here are your spectacles."

Alfredo put them on and the chamber was in darkness. The darkness cracked apart in a glaring line as Uncle Giorgio raised the lid of the furnace unaided. Against the glow Alfredo watched him pick up the little ladle.

He nodded, and Alfredo began.

He started with the saddest requiem he knew, but trying to do as Uncle Giorgio had suggested, and almost at once the salamander emerged, weaving its plaintive sweet piping exquisitely into the music, filling Alfredo's mind with thoughts of the dead sailors, and of their evening concerts, and their gossipy good nature. Together they wept for Benno and his friends while Uncle Giorgio collected the salamander's tears with no more apparent emotion than if he'd been milking a goat. At a suitable moment Alfredo prolonged the note and modulated into the psalm. The salamander followed as if it had been expecting the switch.

"They that go down to the sea in ships, and occupy their business in great waters . . ."

Now, unwilled, his mind filled with other memories—himself on the sun-baked hillside, watching the ships going to and fro in the Straits, the *Bonaventura* with the yellow patch on her brown sail, far out across the water . . .

"These men know the works of the Lord and the wonders in the deep. For at his word the stormy wind ariseth . . ."
And now for him the storm music became the churning energies of the mountain, the *Bonaventura* bursting into

flame, the horror and grief with which he'd watched his friends die. *Why?* he asked himself. *Why?*

Another image came into his mind. He saw the mountain, as if from a short distance, but it was now faintly transparent, so that he could see not only the surface but also, dimly, as if through heavy mist, the branching pattern of dark orange streaks that marked the channels of the fiery mass within. There was a boy, himself, standing on the path directly above one of these streaks, staring out to sea, ashen-faced, his mouth open as if to scream. Farther up the slope, at a point where the streak was brightest, there was a dark, cloudy shape, vaguely human but twice the size of a man and veined with fire like the mountain. It had its arms raised in front of it. Fire streamed from its fingers out toward the sea.

The mountain seemed to come closer as the boy turned, so that now Alfredo was looking over his own imagined shoulder. Beyond him he watched a mule picking its way down between the vines with Uncle Giorgio slumped and exhausted in the saddle.

All this in his mind's eye. At the same time he could feel the salamander's fear and sorrow, and with his outward eyes could see Uncle Giorgio leaning forward to harvest its tears, and he felt he understood why the creature wept so. The sorrow was for him, Alfredo. The fear was for him. They were emotions he could share, human.

He stopped where the storm music ended, and the salamander sank beneath the surface. Alfredo stood with his eyes closed, swaying, paralyzed with horror and dread. If he could have moved he would have tried to rush from the room, despite the locked door.

He hadn't been thinking that! He hadn't! He hadn't!

It hadn't come from inside him!

He'd been doing exactly what he'd been told, trying to sing as if he truly, truly believed that it was the mountain that had destroyed the *Bonaventura* and Uncle Giorgio had tried to stop it.

Or had he? Perhaps . . .

A hand gripped his elbow.

"You still sing with too much feeling," said Uncle Giorgio's voice. "See how you have exhausted yourself."

Alfredo managed to open his eyes. Everything was black. With a shaking hand he removed his spectacles and saw only the dim light of the lantern. The lid of the furnace was closed.

"I . . . I tried," he muttered. "I couldn't help it. I felt so sad."

Uncle Giorgio sighed.

"What is done, is done," he said. "Nothing will undo it. . . ." And then, with an irritated click of the tongue, "Well, we had best not attempt the chant until you are rested. Come to my study half an hour before supper. Meanwhile, learn what you can. You may go."

Alfredo stood dazed, bewildered. That sigh. And the few words after . . . That hadn't been playacting, pretending. But how could that be the voice of the monster the salamander had shown him?

The rattle of the lock broke into his trance. Uncle Giorgio took him by the arm and led him out of the room.

"You had best go and lie down," he said. "Can you manage the stairs on your own? I have work to do here still."

"Yes . . . yes . . . I was just dizzy. I'm all right now."

"Good boy."

Alfredo staggered off along the passage. Before he reached the stair he heard the lock rattle again behind him.

CHAPTER NINE

H

E LEFT THE HOUSE BY THE FRONT DOOR. THE shock of the midmorning sun halted him on the steps. He sank down and sat there with his head in his hands, gasping and shuddering, reliving over and over the thing the salamander had shown him, picking at it with his mind, trying to tease out some clue whether it was the truth, or whether perhaps he had misread it, or whether it really was, as Uncle Giorgio had told him, only an echo of some hidden nightmare of his own.

After a while he rose and, as if trying to leave all those horrors behind him, turned north alongside the façade and followed an overgrown driveway into the wood beyond. Yes, of course, he thought vaguely, once there would have been the gentry's carriages coming and going to and from the house, but none seemed to have used this way for many years. A couple hundred yards into the woods he found out why. The driveway was completely blocked by a mass of soft gray rock twice as high as a man.

Still half in the trance of shock, he stood and stared at it. At first his mind seemed empty, as if the storm of horror that had swept through him had whirled everything away as it went, leaving clear stillness behind, like the morning he had woken from his fever. Thoughts stole back into that emptiness, arranging themselves neatly in their places, making a pattern that when it was finished would tell him what kind of man Uncle Giorgio really was. Everything depended on that, everything.

The rock—it was lava, he guessed—had spewed from the erupting mountain, flowing molten down the slope and solidifying here. Did that tell him anything?

Well, yes, perhaps. It was like the *Bonaventura* all over again. Had Uncle Giorgio for some reason failed to prevent it from happening, Master of the Mountain though he was? Or had he wanted to be alone in his aloneness, with no more comings and goings of gentry in their carriages, and so *caused* it to happen?

And something else. Those gentry . . . the empty stalls in the church . . . were they afraid to worship alongside him . . . ? The priest was afraid of him. . . . The people in the square wouldn't look at him. . . . Did they hate him as well as fear him? Suppose he was truly the kind of man the salamander had shown Alfredo . . . Oh, yes, they would have cause!

Mother and Father—certainly they'd been afraid. . . .

(*"You're not going to let him wear it?"*

"Better than not letting him.")

Had they hated him too? Had they known what he was?

Yes, and that might be why the two brothers had quarreled. Father had seen the kind of Master Uncle Giorgio would become and hadn't liked it, and (of course) had said

so. Anger was in their blood, like the anger of the mountain, ancient, brooding, unappeasable. It was not like the
frozen lava that blocked the driveway—it did not cool.

Then why had Alfredo's parents let him wear such a
giver's gift?

Those snatches of conversation heard through the
kitchen door. *"The mountain must have its Master. That is
the one thing on which we have ever been able to agree."*
And Alfredo was the last of the di Salas in whom the blood
ran true. . . . Thousands upon thousands of innocent lives
might be lost if there was no one to control the mountain's
rages. To Father that would have been more important
than any family quarrel. So, despite everything, he had invited Uncle Giorgio to the christenings of his sons. And allowed Alfredo to accept the gift.

But surely Alfredo's parents would never have given him
up, as a child, to a man they feared and hated, however
great the promised destiny. Of course not. *"He must make
up his own mind when he is old enough to understand."*
So . . .

As the possibility flooded through him the storm came
back. The gray lava flow and the silent shadowy wood
seemed to sway and heave. He staggered and fell forward
onto the rock, and clung there, gasping with the shock of
knowledge. He could not face it. He could not face it.
Could it truly be as he had imagined? Could it?

Slowly his shudderings eased, but he still lay clutching the rock. There was a kind of comfort in it. Once it
had flowed molten in the heart of the mountain, and the
salamanders had swum in its currents. Even now, he

discovered, it was not truly inert. It was still, as it were, veined with the memories of fire. And along those veins, faintly, from far away, he could hear the salamanders singing. They were singing to him, showing him something. Somehow he forced his inward eyes, so far screwed tight shut, to open and look.

He saw through the eyes of a boy sitting in the vestry of the cathedral, less than a month gone by, full of the kindly heat of Father's ovens and the glory of the music he was about to sing. He felt as that boy had felt, felt again the appalling eruption into that peace of the full madness of fire. This was no mere memory. He saw and felt it in the same fashion as with the salamander's help he had just now watched the scene on the mountainside. The cathedral walls were dimly transparent, as were the houses beyond, so that through this cloudy mass he could make out the very street on which the bakery stood, and the inn a little way down on the other side. At an upper window of the inn stood a known shape, a manlike thing, too large for a man, and darkly glowing with inner fire. The Master of the Mountain raised his arms. The fire burst from his fingers and streamed across the street. The bakery exploded into flame.

The vision faded and the singing of the salamanders dwindled away.

"If asked they will tell you the truth."

". . . the truth that the salamander tells you will be contaminated with apparent meanings, which are in fact no more than echoes of your own hopes and fears."

Which? Hadn't he just been thinking of what might have

caused the fire, so the vision was only the echo of that thought?

And how could the salamanders know what had happened in the bakehouse, eight days' journey away to the north?

Oh, for some proof, something outside himself, something the salamanders hadn't told him, something he could see and touch!

There was a movement close beside him and a hand fell on his shoulder, and at the same moment he heard a soft, bubbling sound, anxious and querying, a voice from a human throat, but meaningless. Whoever it was moved sharply away as he pushed himself over. Toni was standing a few feet from him, clearly worried and puzzled, but still poised to run.

Alfredo pulled himself together and managed to smile, but Toni backed off as he rose.

"Would you like to try the recorder again?" said Alfredo, miming the action of playing.

Toni nodded eagerly, so Alfredo led the way back to the house with Toni following in little hesitant rushes behind. Just before they came out of the wood he gave an anxious mutter, and gestured to his right when Alfredo turned to see what the problem was. Apparently he preferred to use a barely visible track that led off through the trees toward the back of the house.

"All right," said Alfredo reassuringly. "I'll get the recorder and meet you in the rose garden. Like yesterday."

Again he mimed playing, and pointed south beyond the

house. Toni nodded even more vigorously and darted off along the track.

The recorder was one of a set of four. Alfredo tried another, whose A was painfully sharp, but the next one was in tune, so he took it with the one he'd played yesterday. Toni was already waiting for him in the rose garden. He put one of the recorders down on the bench and moved away round the fountain. Eagerly Toni rushed in, grabbed the recorder and came and faced him across the empty basin. So they stood and played, each for the other and both for the music.

Alfredo started with the song they had played yesterday. Toni joined him, in unison for the first few bars, but then, and without any apparent effort, harmonizing as though he had known and played the music all his life. It was the same when they moved on to other songs and even suitable bits of cathedral music, some of it difficult enough for Alfredo himself to have trouble with. When that happened Toni stopped him and confidently played the notes as they should have gone. Clearly he had no need of a salamander charm around his neck. He had been born with the gift of music in him, already unlocked.

After a while Alfredo paused to rest, but Toni played happily on, only stopping when he saw Alfredo put his recorder to his lips again. Cautiously, ready to stop at the first flutter of a fiery wing, he started on the music of the Persian chant. Stumbling several times, he played it right through. Toni watched him, frowning. *What kind of weird music is this?* he was thinking, as obviously as if he'd spoken.

All at once his face cleared, and before the last note faded away he had his recorder to his lips. He played the chant easily, without any mistakes. Under the touch of his fingers the music began to make sense. Before he reached the first repetition the air beside him shimmered, and one of the Angels of Fire was standing at his shoulder, visible in the glare of midafternoon as a kind of solidifying of the strong sunlight, an immense presence, an elemental power.

Alfredo opened his mouth to shout a warning, but stopped himself, afraid to interrupt the music now that the thing was there. Toni must have seen his reaction and, still playing, turned to face the Angel and stared up, seemingly unafraid, into its lightning-loaded eyes. The Angel bowed its head in a gesture of respect, and waited until the chant ended. Then it reached out with a flaming finger and traced what might have been a series of symbols, or fiery letters, in an arching line above Toni's head. That done, it moved back a pace, bowed and vanished.

Toni stood staring at the place where it had been and began to weep. He didn't seem to have changed, as far as Alfredo could see. He had the same hesitant stance of an idiot, the same lopsided down-drawing of the jaw. But then he turned, blinking through his tears, saw Alfredo, and with his half-crouching gait came round the basin toward him. When he stopped he didn't seem poised to run. Instead he held out his recorder to Alfredo and withdrew it, clutching it against his chest.

Please, please may I keep it?

Why not? Why cause the poor man yet more misery? It

wouldn't be missed, surely. The recorder case hadn't been opened for years.

"Of course," said Alfredo, nodding and gesturing toward him with outspread palms. He hid his own recorder behind his back, pointed toward the house and put a finger to his lips.

"Don't let my uncle know you've got it," he said. "Don't play it near the house. I think we'd better not play any more now. I've got to go and sing to my uncle soon."

Toni nodded and hid the recorder under his shirt. Alfredo started off toward the house, with Toni shambling along only half a pace behind him, but as soon as the buildings came in sight slipping off along one of his private paths. Alfredo guessed he had a cache somewhere for his special treasures. He himself went round by the courtyard and into the kitchen, wondering whether he should tell Annetta what had happened. Not yet, he decided; not until he knew a bit more.

The wind had shifted, altering the draft in the flue. It wasn't serious, but for something to do he put a small oak log on the fire and fiddled with the damper in the door. Before he'd finished Toni came in and, ignoring Alfredo, settled at the table. Annetta stopped what she was doing to give him some food, and Alfredo took advantage of her absence from the stove to get at the flue damper. He turned back to the room already raising his hand in greeting to Toni, but the gesture stopped, half made. For several thudding heartbeats he stood staring.

Toni was already intent on his food, but this time wasn't

crouched protectively over it. He sat sideways at the table, straddling the bench, tearing a piece off his bread to dip in his bowl. Oh, how well Alfredo knew that pose! That was how Father sat, and Uncle Giorgio, too. Normally, of course, they used chairs, where the oddity wasn't so obvious, but he'd often seen Father sitting like that in inns and other places where there were only benches.

He realized Annetta was looking at him.

"He sits just the way my father used to sit!" he blurted. "My uncle does it too!"

She nodded calmly.

"My uncle's son? My cousin?"

She nodded again.

Yes, of course! That was why Toni had been able to summon the Angel! The mind might be damaged, but the blood ran true. . . .

Another pulse of understanding. Yes again, this woman to live in his house, to bear his children—of course Uncle Giorgio would want her dumb, another barrier round his aloneness, his secrets. Perhaps some of those children would inherit the defect—what of it? One son who could speak, and sing to the salamander, would be enough. Nothing else mattered.

Only there was also a defect in the father's seed. His own seed. He could sire child after child on whatever woman would let him, and he would finish up with a household of idiots—horrible! A punishment, a judgment, for what he had done and become? No wonder he had spoken of it with such anger and contempt.

Alfredo pulled himself together, walked round the

table and put his arm round Toni's shoulders and hugged him. Toni looked up at him with a surprised smile, hesitated and offered him his piece of bread. Alfredo tore off a morsel, dipped it in the bowl and ate. He looked across at Annetta and saw that she was smiling, though there were tears on her cheeks. At that moment the big clock in the hallway clanked the hour. There wasn't much time before he'd need to go and sing the chant for Uncle Giorgio, so he gave Toni another hug, then went back round the table and hugged Annetta. She bent and kissed him on the forehead.

Halfway up the stairs he realized that his feelings had changed. He had finally stopped trying to love and trust Uncle Giorgio. It wasn't because of anything the salamanders had told him, or what Uncle Giorgio might or might not have done to Alfredo's family, or his friends on the *Bonaventura*—there was still no way he could be sure about things like that. It was because of the way he had treated Annetta and Toni, and what he had said when Alfredo had asked about them. How could you love someone who spoke like that of his own son, or of the woman who had mothered that son for him?

Perhaps there might have been another Uncle Giorgio— the man Alfredo had glimpsed once, standing troubled at his study window, heard that very morning in a sigh and a few regret-laden words—but he was gone and would not come back. It was, as he himself had said, too late.

And something else. Uncle Giorgio was no longer the only family Alfredo had in the world. He had found a cousin, and an aunt, people who actually felt like family in a way Uncle Giorgio didn't. People it would be possible to love.

But Uncle Giorgio mustn't believe that anything had changed, so he settled into his window and read the words of the chant over and over, and found as he did so that since Toni had played it in the rose garden, the strange music had somehow become familiar and lodged in his mind. As he mouthed the unintelligible syllables they seemed to fit themselves naturally to the notes and cling there. He put the paper aside and whispered them through, half expecting to see the Angels of Fire floating quietly up across the long shadows toward the sunset, but there was only the breeze and the dry herby odors of the southern hills. When it was time he made his way down to Uncle Giorgio's study.

Standing at the door, he paused, once again remembering that Uncle Giorgio could feel the comings and goings of the molten currents in the mountain, and wondering how much else? How closely did he watch? Was he already aware of all that Alfredo had done and seen that afternoon, of the singing of the salamanders in the lava flow, and above all, of the great Angel of Fire in the rose garden? No. Surely he would have done something about the Angel, had he known. . . .

That apart, Alfredo felt both tense and calm. He seemed able to sense that things were moving, moving fast, to whatever place they were going. He had no plan, no idea of what might happen, or what he would then do. The important thing was that when whatever was coming at last did so, it would not be wholly under Uncle Giorgio's control, though he himself might believe it was. Uncle Giorgio had great power, but there were other powers around that were not his to command. Nor was Alfredo. Uncle Giorgio might believe he was completely under his control, but he wasn't. Alfredo had knowledge his uncle knew nothing about, and friends where his uncle believed he had none.

He drew a deep, steadying breath and scratched on the door.

"One! Two! Three! Four!" shrieked the starling, drowning his uncle's answer. He lifted the latch and went in.

Uncle Giorgio seemed unperturbed, indeed, almost eager to see him. He put his book down at once and looked up. "You are rested?" he said. "You have learned what you can?"

"Yes, I think I know it."

"All of it? Well, let us see. Watch me. Stop if I hold up my hand."

Alfredo straightened his shoulders, put his hands behind his back, drew breath and began, singing quietly, as if to himself, concentrating on his memory of the words, sure that the notes were there ready and waiting to hold them. Halfway through the first repeat Uncle Giorgio stopped him and he fell instantly silent, holding the next phrase ready in mind and throat, much as if he'd been holding his breath. The air in the study seemed to crackle, or prickle. His skin crawled. He recognized the nearness of the Angels of Fire.

Uncle Giorgio muttered a few words into the silence. The sensations faded. He nodded to Alfredo to sing on. He did so, and reached the end without further interruption.

111

"Excellent," said Uncle Giorgio. "You have done very well, Alfredo, better than I could have hoped. This chant is not itself in your blood, only the ability to perform it. None of your ancestors, for many generations, since first we came out of Persia and settled on the mountain, had known it. I myself underwent much labor and danger to search it out. I traveled to the farthest East, to the Island of Fire, and there I found the last of those who speak that ancient tongue, and to gain their trust I underwent the Ordeal of Fire, so that they should teach me the chant, and other long-forgotten secrets, which one day you too will know. . . .

"Now, listen. Next Monday is the full moon in Leo, which is one of the three Houses of Fire. Furthermore it falls in the season when Sol is at his strongest. I had not expected you to be ready so soon, but now, on that day, we will perform the Second Great Work, you and I. Before we can do that, though, there is a test to make, which we must do as near to the full moon as we may come, and yet give ourselves time to rest, for the task we must undertake requires strength—strength of body, strength of mind, strength of will. So you must look after yourself, Alfredo—eat well, sleep well, rest. In two days we will go to town so that I may make my new will, and Wednesday you will sing again to the salamander. On Friday, we will make the test, and if that goes well, then on Monday, the Great Work!"

He spoke in his usual slow, precise, slightly grating voice, but his excitement throbbed within it like the fires in the mountain.

"And what then?" he whispered.

"I don't know, Uncle. Is there a Third Great Work?"

"Who knows, Alfredo? Who knows? If a man in our pitiful little lifetime can come to control a mountain, then a man who lives forever might control the innermost fires of the earth!"

He turned away abruptly, snatched a crust from the bowl by the birdcage and fed it through the bars. "One! Two! Three! Four!" screamed the starling, and fell on it.

"Time for us also to go and eat," said Uncle Giorgio, and opened the door.

CHAPTER TEN

ALFREDO WOKE EARLY, DRESSED AND SAT IN THE window, breathing the soft dawn air and letting the early sunlight stream over him. It was all the same as yesterday, the same sun, the same air, the same marvelous view. But everything had changed, himself included. He felt as if he had somehow grown two or three years older during the night. He was no longer a child, letting everything be decided for him by someone else. From now on he was a person who must think and decide and act for himself. From now on he was going to cope for himself with the responsibilities before him, to his dead parents and poor Giorgio, to Annetta and Toni, to himself. Only Uncle Giorgio must go on thinking he was a child, unquestioning and obedient. But he would be wrong.

The week inched by. Alfredo teased obsessively away at the sheet of notes about the salamanders. A few of the more carefully written bits began to make sense: *They have great knowledge, but little power. . . . Of all things concerning fire, though far from the island, they know through the fires within the earth*.... (Ah, so they could after all have known what had happened in the bakehouse.) ... *not things to come ... cannot see into the minds of men ... not like the Angels of Fire, both Lesser and Greater. These have many powers ... One with the Knowledge can command the Lesser Angels, but neither the Greater, nor the sala-manders*. ...

When he had unraveled all he could he started to read his way slowly on through Livius's history. At other times he studied old musical scores and tried to learn some of the easier pieces on the recorder, so that he could teach them to Toni. Or he walked the mountainside, until he could join Toni in the rose garden each afternoon, when for an hour or more they improvised duets together and he could forget about his hopes and his fears. He didn't run away from these. Indeed he tried to face them, mostly when he was sitting in the kitchen before supper while Toni ate and Annetta worked at the stove.

It was easier when they were there, because they re-minded him of what sort of man Uncle Giorgio must be to have used them so, as if they existed entirely for his own purposes, and nothing else mattered. A man like that might well have used and destroyed his own brother with his family, and the crew of the *Bonaventura,* without a thought, simply because it suited him. It didn't *prove* he had — it just made it more likely — and more likely too that he was planning to use Alfredo in the same kind of way. It was going to happen next Monday as part of the Second Great Work.

How could he avoid taking part in that work? Run away? Where? Who would dare help him hide from the Master of the Mountain? How could he be sure his uncle didn't have the power to find him, wherever he hid? And then he would have betrayed part of his own secret knowledge—and his one hope lay in his uncle's not suspecting how much he knew. Kill himself, then? If the worst came to the worst, perhaps, but how? If he could find a cliff somewhere to throw himself over . . .

No. There must be a better way, if only he could think of it.

On the Tuesday morning Annetta came to his room early and laid out his church clothes for him. After breakfast he sang the chant again for Uncle Giorgio, who this time muttered a few words almost as soon as he'd begun. There were no interruptions from the Angels. Then they rode down the hill to the town. Uncle Giorgio stopped at a large, newish house opposite the church, where they were evidently expected, for a groom from the inn was waiting for them and led the mules away. Uncle Giorgio was raising his cane to rap on the door when it was opened by a wheezing old man in black, wearing a tatty wig, who showed them through a musty hallway, opened a door and announced, or rather muttered, "Signor Giorgio di Sala with the young gentleman, sir," then stood aside for them and slipped away.

Just as they went into the room Uncle Giorgio gripped Alfredo's shoulder and leaned heavily on it. He tottered forward.

A man rose from behind a table and started to greet them, but checked himself, stared for a moment and rushed round, pulled out a chair and helped Uncle Giorgio to settle into it, then went back to his place. He was younger than Alfredo would have expected, but stout and with heavy, dark features. His manner, like the priest's last Sunday, was both fawning and wary.

"Signor di Sala," he said. "I am much honored. You are . . . you are not well?"

"I have been stronger," said Uncle Giorgio dismissively. "You received my note?"

"Indeed, indeed. And this is the young gentleman who is now to be your heir?"

"My nephew, Alfredo," said Uncle Giorgio. "His parents died tragically a month ago, and he is now in my care. The last, for the moment, of our line. Alfredo, this is my friend Signor Pozzarelli, who looks after the legal side of our affairs. You will have much to do with him in time to come."

"Indeed, indeed. I am gratified to meet you, Signor Alfredo," said Signor Pozzarelli as they shook hands. "But let us hope it will be many years before that is the case."

"We are in God's hands, Signor Pozzarelli," said Uncle Giorgio. "And as you see I have not been well. The journey to fetch my nephew taxed my strength, and I was near to death by the time I returned. I am not yet fully recovered, and the malady could strike again at any time. We must put my earthly affairs in order without delay."

"Your earthly . . . ?" Signor Pozzarelli began, and stopped himself. "Er . . . hum . . . a little wine in honor of the occasion? Now, let me see, let me see . . ."

He rang a silver handbell, then fussed with papers on his table, recovering his composure. Uncle Giorgio watched him, smiling thinly. Alfredo was puzzled. He had a feeling Uncle Giorgio was teasing the attorney, but why was he pretending to be ill and mouthing these pious phrases about his own death if in a few day's time he was going to start living forever? And what had Signor Pozzarelli been going to say when he stopped himself?

A servant woman came in with a tray—glasses, a wine flask and a jug. Signor Pozzarelli poured two glasses of wine and glanced at Uncle Giorgio.

"A little for my nephew—as you say, in honor of the occasion," said Uncle Giorgio, still with that teasing note, so the attorney poured a few sips for Alfredo and filled the larger glasses from the jug with what turned out to be lime water, cool and fresh. The wine was dark and sweet—the best in the attorney's cellar, Alfredo guessed.

Signor Pozzarelli drew a chair to the table for Alfredo, picked up a double sheet of parchment and cleared his throat.

"The terms, as you suggested, are the same as for the last will—nineteen years ago, I see—save of course for the beneficiary. The list of your properties has been kept up to date, as you know, and can simply be transferred to the new will. And there is the matter of a guardian still to be settled. Last time my father had the honor . . ."

"Your respected father is now almost as old as I am, and we must look to the future. I suggest that this time it should be yourself, if you will be so kind as to take up the burden of my nephew's earthly affairs. All else of course is in eternal hands, those hands which finally take care of all things, both earthly and beyond."

"Of course, of course," agreed Signor Pozzarelli hastily. "I shall be much honored by the task."

This time Alfredo got it. Beneath Uncle Giorgio's teasing tone there was something else, a note of threat, quiet but confident. And beneath the attorney's gabbled reply there was awareness of that threat, and fear of it. And Uncle Giorgio hadn't said the obvious "earthly and heavenly," but used the strange phrase "earthly and beyond." He was talking not of the justice of God, but of the powers of the Master of the Mountain, which his nephew would inherit. No attorney in his right mind would be tempted to swindle even a child who possessed those powers.

Signor Pozzarelli wrote briefly on the document, then read it through in a solemn voice. Though it was quite short, it was mostly incomprehensible. The only thing that was clear to Alfredo was that just three people were named in it, Uncle Giorgio, who was making the will; Signor Pozzarelli, who was to be guardian; and Alfredo himself, who was getting everything. There was nothing for Annetta, nothing to take care of poor Toni, Uncle Giorgio's own son. Of course Alfredo would look after them, but how could anyone be certain of that? If only for form's sake surely . . . But no. Uncle Giorgio didn't think like that.

When he'd finished reading, Signor Pozzarelli rang his bell again, and the clerk and a gardener came to witness Uncle Giorgio's signature. The gardener was unable to write his name, so signed with a thumbprint. Uncle Giorgio gave each of them a silver coin and rose as they left. Alfredo realized that Signor Pozzarelli was looking expectantly at him. Alfredo pulled himself together.

"I must . . . must thank my uncle for his great generosity," he stammered. "I, er, will try to prove worthy of my inheritance and . . . and our name."

"I have no doubt that that will prove to be the case," said Uncle Giorgio, still with the same odd tone, as if the words had an extra meaning that only he knew. He signed to Alfredo, who helped him stand and then took some of his weight while Signor Pozzarelli showed them out of the house with obvious relief, bowing his farewells several times more than was necessary.

Uncle Giorgio seemed to recover as soon as the door closed.

"Lawyers are capable of infinite delay," he remarked. "There is no harm in persuading one that the case may be urgent."

He sounded really pleased with himself. He stood for a while on the doorstep, like a cat purring in the strong noon sun, while Alfredo once again wondered what it must be like to have everyone you met terrified of you. But Uncle Giorgio actually seemed to enjoy it. Strange.

Now he stalked off toward the inn, but started to lean on his stick before they reached it. Alfredo had been expecting that they would simply collect the mules and ride home, but the landlord was waiting at the door, bowing and smiling but still giving the impression that he would have preferred to run and hide in his darkest cellar.

"I trust the signor is in good health," he gabbled.

"Feeling my age, feeling my age," said Uncle Giorgio,

speaking almost affably. "I shall need your arm up the stairs, I fear."

The landlord helped him climb slowly to a room overlooking the harbor, where a table was laid for two.

Uncle Giorgio straightened as soon as they were alone.

"A feast in celebration of the occasion," he said genially.

Alfredo's heart sank. How could he eat a feast of celebration with this man whom he now believed to be a monster, a murderer? Sitting in the attorney's office, pretending to be honored and grateful about what his uncle was doing for him—that wasn't difficult. In a grim sense he'd almost enjoyed it, because each little deception of Uncle Giorgio became part of his secret knowledge. It was all right eating together up at the house, where often his uncle read throughout the meal and scarcely said a word, so that they might just as well have been eating in separate rooms, and where even when they talked their words seemed to be full of secret meanings. But here, like this? He thought of name-days at home, the joy, the family love, Mother's pride in what she'd prepared for the occasion. That had been true celebration, not this. The food would be sawdust in his mouth, tasteless and unswallowable, and he must pretend to enjoy it.

No, he would not think like that. Soon, soon, before next Monday, he would find proof of what the salamanders had told him. And then . . . then somehow—something deep and savage stirred in him—then he would take vengeance.

They sat and the meal was brought, olives and bread and oil, of course, and grilled sardines caught fresh that morning, and a salad of wild leaves from the mountain, and a tender young pullet roasted on a bed of herbs, and a strange, sweet custard, and three kinds of wine, and lime water better than the attorney's—indeed the sort of meal Mother would have prepared for a name-day.

Alfredo settled down to enjoy it, savoring every mouthful with the thought of his vengeance. Vengeance, he discovered, makes an excellent savor. So he ate with gusto until Uncle Giorgio pulled him up.

"We must feed you up but not make you ill," he said, lightly enough—but still Alfredo seemed to hear the undertone of another kind of meaning. This time, though, he could guess what it was. To Uncle Giorgio each mouthful he ate, each sip he drank, each breath he drew, was not for his own pleasure, but a preparation for next Monday and his mysterious destiny.

He thought about this as they rode up the hill and wondered if he could starve himself until he was too weak to do whatever his uncle expected of him on Monday. Not easily, if he was watched all the time as he ate. But . . .

That evening, sitting in the kitchen and watching Annetta preparing supper, he wondered where her loyalties really lay. He decided to take the risk.

"Annetta?"

She turned from the stove, eyebrows raised.

"Can you give me something to make me a little bit sick? Not really sick, just so I don't have to do something. Only for a morning—I can't explain. He'd see through it if I was just shamming sick."

She frowned for a moment, glanced at Toni and stared at her hands. Alfredo could see her thinking *What if the master found out?* He sighed with relief when she straightened, looked him firmly in the eye and nodded.

She laid her spoon down, crossed to her store cupboard and reached to the back of a high shelf for a small lidded pot. She fetched a mug, and her kettle from the back of the stove, took a leaf out of the pot, put it in the mug and mimed filling the mug from the kettle. She pointed at the kitchen clock and made a slow circle in the air. *Wait for an hour.* She then pretended to drink the contents of the mug.

That done, she tipped the leaf out onto the table and added two more from the pot, rinsed the mug carefully and laid it to drain. She pointed at the leaves, held up a finger, clutched her stomach and pretended to retch into her hands. Two fingers, and this time she was in serious pain and vomiting onto the floor. Three fingers, and she started to curl up in agony, then straightened, smiling.

"One leaf would make me a bit ill, and two properly ill, and three I'd be really sick," said Alfredo. "If I took just one, how long would it be before I threw up?"

She pointed at the clock again, held up her finger and wrapped her other hand round the bottom half of it. *Half an hour.*

"And how long before I got better?"

This time she held up four fingers. Then she poured

water into a bowl, washed her hands, threw the water away and rinsed out the bowl.

"Thank you, Annetta," he said. "I won't use it unless I have to—there may be another way."

He took the leaves up to his room and hid them in a book. Following Annetta's example, he washed his hands carefully before he came back downstairs.

"A light supper after our midday feast," said Uncle Giorgio pleasantly enough. "I think we are both too tired for talk."

Alfredo agreed, with relief, and took up his book. They did not speak again until they said goodnight. That was Tuesday.

⚗

All night Alfredo dreamed restlessly of his vengeance. He woke early, and discovered that his confidence had somehow thinned in the night, as if it had become part of the now forgotten dreams. Yesterday his decision to trust the salamanders, his new hatred of his uncle and his determination to take his vengeance if he got the chance had seemed fixed and certain. Now both trust and determination had become doubtful, and without them what right had he to hatred? And even suppose, miraculously, he found the proof he needed, he could see no way forward, and was heavily aware of how little his power was, how few and small his secrets, compared to all that Uncle Giorgio knew from his study, and his long Mastership of the mountain. Fear had returned—not full-fledged panic, but a steady underlying apprehension, a feeling that he was picking his way along a narrow track with a precipitous drop below, and dared not look down.

The sun was just rising as he went out into the silvery sweet dawn, not with any purpose, simply needing to be away from the house and all it meant. As before he found himself wandering along the overgrown driveway until his way was blocked by the old lava flow.

He gazed a while, unthinking, and then, though it was still full of the chill of night, stretched himself out on it, molded his body to it, made himself part of it, imagined himself seeping down through its hidden veins, feeling his way toward the distant central fires. Faintly now he thought he could hear the singing of the salamanders.

Oh, what is going to happen to me? he asked them.

The singing paused and resumed, but muddled and uncertain. Like a fever dream. Whoever had written the notes he had found had been right— *Nobody, not even we ourselves,* the salamanders seemed to be telling him, *knows what is going to happen, not until it happens. Till then there is no certainty about it, no truth for us to tell.*

He wasn't disappointed. In his heart he had known this to be so, just as he knew, too, that it was no use asking them what Uncle Giorgio was planning. They couldn't see into the minds of men. But the singing of the salamanders, and the fact that he could hear them, were comforting in themselves, so he lay where he was for a while, and then went back to the house for breakfast. As soon as they had eaten Uncle Giorgio took him down to the furnace room.

Alfredo went reluctantly. He wasn't in the mood for grief. Doubt and fear left no room for it. But sing he must, sing the music of sorrow.

"By the waters of Babylon I sat down and wept . . ."

For once in his life the music didn't seem to be part of him. Some of the adult choristers had been like that, singing their way through the services by rote, steady on the note from endless repetition, while their minds were on other things—a woman they were keen on, a bit of gossip they'd heard, their next meal. Nevertheless the salamander rose and wept. The sorrow was in the music, as Uncle Giorgio had said. That was all it needed, and its own grief, the grief of exile, which was real, and apparently unending.

How did it come to be here, in this prison? he wondered.

Alfredo hadn't intended to ask the question—to question it at all—but it answered. As they sang on together he saw it swimming in the fiery currents of the mountain with its comrades, none of them yet fully grown. They were exploring, as young creatures tend to, the edges of their territory, daring each other to see how far they could go. A music reached them, strange and powerful. The rock above them split open and the current that carried them welled into the world above. Still the music held them, compelling them upward. The salamander raised its head above the surface and looked around. Something seized it from behind and lifted it clear of the molten rock into the killing cold of air.

It had struggled desperately, but it was gripped firm between two meshes of metal and was carried to where two huge creatures were waiting—Alfredo recognized these as a pair of horses or mules—with a large object slung on

126

poles between them. An arm reached from beneath the salamander and opened the lid of the object, which was filled with glowing coals. It was lowered into the life-giving heat and there released. As the lid was closed upon it it could hear, close by, two human voices, loud with anger, and farther off, the horrified wails of its comrades mourning its loss.

Then darkness and endless jolting, and the embers cooling, cooling, until it lost consciousness. And finally waking to find itself in this furnace, also then filled with coals which were just enough to keep it alive, and were constantly replenished until out of its own natural process it had transmuted what was fed to it into the true stuff of the sun in which it now lived, and had lived for thirty long years.

It was an account of cruelty and horror and loss. The salamander wept, but Alfredo did not weep with it or for it. Deliberately he used his thoughts of vengeance as a kind of harness to hold his tears and his voice in check, to stay dry-eyed, to sing the notes clearly and truly. So as he watched Uncle Giorgio coolly harvesting the tears of his prisoner, his resolve seemed to harden. That his uncle should treat the wonderful creature so! And Toni, too, and Annetta. And probably, all too probably, Alfredo himself.

Yet still it was not quite enough. Some final, definite proof must be found, and then he would have vengeance on his uncle, and part of that vengeance would be somehow to free the salamander, take it back up the mountain and release it into the fiery torrents that were its home.

At last Uncle Giorgio closed the lid of the furnace and

removed his spectacles. Alfredo did the same and wiped his eyes.

"That is better," said Uncle Giorgio approvingly. "But there is still too much feeling. You must not exhaust yourself so. There is more important work waiting for you."

He tipped the little draught of tears into his phial and started to tap off the molten gold from beneath the furnace. Trying to look as if he were simply waiting for him to finish, Alfredo let his glance wander round the chamber, all dim and shadowy after the furnace glare, in case there was anything here that would help him in his enterprise. Yes, in the corner to his left what looked like the selfsame large lidded iron bucket that Uncle Giorgio had used to carry his captive down the mountain; beside it a similar smaller bucket; and propped behind them a heavy ladle, an instrument like a large pair of tongs, each arm ending in a circular metal grill, and a stout pole with a hook at the center so that two people could carry the buckets between them.

Uncle Giorgio rose from his crouch, holding the little pan into which he had been running the gold from the bottom of the furnace, and put it back on the table. A thin film of still-molten metal covered what he had collected five days ago. Uncle Giorgio turned the full pan over, rapped it sharply with a wooden mallet and pocketed the little ingot that fell out.

Lost in his thoughts of vengeance, Alfredo gazed vaguely at the two pans, one now empty, one half full, as if they, too, might help him somehow to free the salamander, until Uncle Giorgio broke the trance.

"Yes, Alfredo, pure gold. The First Great Work," he purred, and turned to leave.

Alfredo pulled himself together and on the way out took a good look at the door and its lock. Both seemed formidably sturdy. As usual Uncle Giorgio put the key back in his pocket as soon as he had locked the door.

"I have work to do now," he said. "You will be able to amuse yourself until luncheon?"

"Yes, of course, Uncle. I'll go for a walk in the woods. So I don't need to take my hat."

"Good boy."

Alfredo wandered in a seemingly aimless manner out to the driveway in case Uncle Giorgio was watching from the study windows. For a while he simply stood and stared at the lava flow, lying massively inert in the dappled shade. At length he lay down once more, molded his body to the coarse rock and waited. This was not something he could make happen in a hurry, or even coax into happening. A bird fluted and was answered from deep among the trees. A faint breeze blew and died away. And then, slowly, slowly, the mountain drew him into itself as it had done before, and they became one. Far off and faint, he heard the singing of the salamanders.

Again he waited. The music changed, telling him they were aware of his presence. He shaped his question formally in his mind.

You have shown me how my father and my mother and

my brother died, and who killed them. What proof can you give me that what you tell me is true?

The answer came instantly, in a rapid burst of excited song, and he was back in the furnace room, gazing, as he had done barely half an hour ago, at two small rectangular pans, one empty, the second half-full and with a thin molten layer covering the solid metal beneath, and a hand closing round a small gold bar.

That was all, and the salamanders showed him no more.

What did it mean? The answer came like a thunderclap. He lay and forced his mind to do the sums. Five days ago Uncle Giorgio had drawn a pan and a half from the furnace. In those five days enough more matter had passed through the salamander's body to add little more than a film of gold to what was already in the pan. How many such fillings to fill a whole pan? Eight? Call it six, to be on the safe side. Five sixes were thirty, plus half of that was forty-five, so it had taken forty-five days to produce the gold that Uncle Giorgio had drawn the day after his return to Casa di Sala. Perhaps it was less. Call it forty, to be on the safe side again. And perhaps he hadn't drawn any in the last few days before he left, so call it thirty-five. He must have been five weeks away from Casa di Sala, at least.

But sixteen days after the fire in the bakery Uncle Giorgio had told the priests in the cathedral that he had come posthaste on hearing the news of the tragedy. That can't have been true. A house fire in a distant northern city? Not the sort of news that travels fast. But suppose Alfredo's father had made arrangements for his brother to be told at once if anything should happen to him—in that case how long for the news to get to Sicily? Say five days. That would leave eleven days for Uncle Giorgio to travel north, setting up the elaborate arrangements for their escape route. Yes, it could just be done.

So if Uncle Giorgio had left Sicily only on hearing the news of his brother's death, he couldn't have been away from Casa di Sala for more than twenty-two days, at the outside. How much gold would have gathered in the bottom of the furnace in that time? Not enough to fill one little pan, nothing like. So he had been away from Casa di Sala much longer than he said.

He must have started out at least a fortnight before the fire.

Why?

Because he needed to be in the city for several days before it, to set up his plan, to find his informant in the cathedral, to hire the first boat to be ready and waiting to take them to the island, to rent an upper room at the inn across the road from the bakery, and so on. And then, on that final dreadful evening, to go to the room and summon his powers as Master of the Mountain, and draw the fires of the bakehouse ovens bursting out of their fire beds to burn and destroy. And all the while the salamander's gold was settling slowly into the bottom of the furnace, until there was enough there for him on his return to tap off one full pan and half another one.

What if the priests had decided to perform the operation sooner? Or later? (That was why he had needed the informant—one of the vergers or canons—to tell him that kind of thing.) Sooner, and he'd have had to invent some story about being already traveling in Italy when he got the news, in case Alfredo asked. Later and he'd have needed to claim Alfredo before the decision had been made, but for different reasons that wouldn't have suited him as well. What he'd wanted was what had actually happened, that he should intervene at the last possible moment to save Alfredo from the operation, thus binding his nephew to him with ties of gratitude and trust, with the tears of the salamander keeping him alive but losing their potency day by day.

Perhaps the priests had waited longer than he'd expected, and he'd hung on till what he'd thought was the last safe moment. But he had miscalculated the time it would take for the *Bonaventura* to sail the final leg home, and so had indeed come very near death for Alfredo's sake.

Yes. Proof. Proof at last. And the salamanders told the truth.

Long after the singing of the salamanders had died away Alfredo lay where he was, thinking it through. But the cold fire in the rock did not die. Instead it seemed to gather itself together and flow upward, out through the surface, into his innermost body and become part of him. Thus Alfredo di Sala discovered his ancient inheritance of anger. The anger of fire. His birthright. Yes.

Now he was at last unshakeably certain what he must do. The whole of his life had narrowed suddenly to a single purpose: to take vengeance on Uncle Giorgio for the murder of his family. He still had no idea how he was going to achieve it, but nothing else mattered till it was done.

Still he lay where he was, feeding on the strength of the

mountain. He must become like the mountain himself, standing calmly above the Straits, flanked with peaceful olive groves and vineyards, hiding its roiling inner furies until the time came for them in their turn to burst out and burn and destroy. Yes, it was like that that he would destroy Uncle Giorgio. With fire.

Now he must think how.

He began with the freeing of the salamander. Finding a way into the furnace room was the first serious problem. He pushed himself up off the rock and went and poked around among the outbuildings, looking for tools with which to break down the door. He found a crowbar too heavy for him to wield and an even heavier wooden mallet. Toni could have managed them if he could be made to understand what was needed, and if Annetta would have let him, but it wouldn't be fair for Alfredo to ask her, knowing what Uncle Giorgio might do in his fury when he found his salamander gone. For himself, he was prepared to take the consequences, but just freeing the salamander wasn't enough. He wanted more than that. Uncle Giorgio must be destroyed, and know as he perished by whom, and why, and that the salamander was free once more.

He was in the stables, thinking about this, when he found the harness for the three mules. There were several sets, used for different purposes. Above them, on a couple of brackets, lay a long contraption, two poles joined at intervals by shorter ones, hinged at the joints so that when not in use the poles could be laid side by side. A heavy iron hoop dangled from them. He could guess what he was looking at. He had seen this sort of thing down at the harbor. It was slung between two horses standing fore and aft and was used for carrying a load too heavy for a single animal—yes, this was how Uncle Giorgio had carried the salamander down from the mountain. The hoop was the right size to hold the big pot he had seen in the furnace chamber. More proof, he realized. The salamander had told him the truth, about its own capture, at least. How else could it have known about these objects, out here in the stables? Not that it mattered.

What mattered now was that this was how Alfredo was going to carry the salamander back. Not at once, though. When the time was right. First, though, there was the problem of getting through this coming Monday without confronting whatever destiny it was that Uncle Giorgio had chosen for him. He got no farther with this before it was time to return to the house for luncheon.

CHAPTER ELEVEN

SURREPTITIOUSLY ALFREDO STUDIED UNCLE Giorgio while they ate. He was reading a book, but not in his usual steady, absorbed fashion. Instead he seemed to be flipping impatiently to and fro, reading a page or two, and then skipping to somewhere else. Alfredo realized that his uncle must be just as much on edge about the next few days as he was himself. Then, abruptly, he closed the book and pushed it aside.

"I hope you spent a pleasant morning," he said.

Alfredo was taken by surprise. He had in fact been thinking about how he was going to manage both mules on the mountain path. Toni was very good with the mules, and could take the lead one, but it would have to be arranged so that Uncle Giorgio didn't find out that he'd done so, and again, what could he say to Annetta to persuade her to let him? He stammered for a moment, then said the obvious thing.

"You told me to rest, so I went up to my room and read for a bit. Then I went out and just wandered about. I'm not used to having so much time. At the cathedral we mostly did lessons when we weren't singing. And you said I mustn't sing at all while I'm here."

"Soon you shall sing all you wish. As for lessons, there is no suitable school in the town, but I will make inquiries for a tutor for you. You have something else on your mind, I think."

He'd noticed! He'd guessed. Thoroughly rattled now, Alfredo again stammered the first thing that came into his mind.

"I, er—I know it's none of my business, but what's going to happen to Toni? I mean . . ."

"You need not trouble yourself about Toni. Such cases do not survive much into manhood. The idiot is not long for this world."

His own son! Alfredo was appalled and shocked by the casual tone.

"That's sad," he managed to say.

"Nonsense! It is much better so! Much better!"

This time the tone was far from casual. The words were spoken with spitting venom. Uncle Giorgio snatched up his book and started to read, leaving Alfredo stiff and chilly with understanding. Nineteen years ago Uncle Giorgio had made his previous will, naming somebody as his single heir—Toni, of course, new born, and before anyone had realized what he was. But they must have known soon after that, and from then on Uncle Giorgio had begun to detest the mere existence of the son who had failed to be what he wanted, and he longed to see him dead.

In that case why hadn't he done away with him years ago? He was perfectly capable of it. Because . . . because

Toni had been all there was, until Alfredo came. But now, especially after next Monday . . . Once again he remembered the risks Uncle Giorgio had taken to get him here, not for family love or duty or anything like that, but because for his own purposes he truly needed to have him. He remembered the strange, intense look with which his uncle had stared at him on the mountain. Even then Alfredo had guessed at the need. On this coming Monday the need would be fulfilled. And after that he would no longer have any possible use for Toni. So Toni was not long for this world.

Alfredo munched his way through the rest of the meal, barely tasting a mouthful. When at last it was over he went up to his room to rest out the first heat of the afternoon. He tried to read, but his mind wouldn't apply itself to anything but his problems, where it skittered uselessly to and fro between them. *I must talk to Annetta again,* he decided. *I must tell her everything. Then she can make up her own mind what to do.*

Long before the heat was any less he crept downstairs, took the recorder from its case and went out to the rose garden. Toni was already there, sitting on the bench playing softly—not anything Alfredo had taught him but a strange little tune that he seemed to be making up as he went along, because every now and then he would stop, go back to an earlier phrase and alter what he'd done before, fiddling with it several times until he was satisfied.

Alfredo leaned on the balustrade, watching and listening. After a while Toni seemed to be happy with what he'd invented and started again from the beginning. Alfredo took out his recorder and joined in. Toni looked up, but didn't stop playing. The tune was trickier than Alfredo had realized, with unexpected time-changes. It was the sort of music that makes you want to dance, but you'd need to be a clever dancer not to make a fool of yourself. Alfredo made a lot of mistakes, but Toni held the tune firm all the way through. The last notes died into the breathless air and they laughed together.

Alfredo went down the steps and sat beside Toni on the bench.

"You made that up yourself," he said, pointing at Toni as he asked the question.

Toni nodded and tapped his chest. Obviously he'd understood, but from the way Annetta talked to him and about him he'd always understood a few simple things. He was probably still like that. The Angel of Fire hadn't cured him, hadn't disentangled whatever was wrong with his mind, but it had done something else, even more important. It had set him free, freed his spirit, his soul, freed them from his terror of the world and his shame of what he was. It had given him a life worth living.

Alfredo thought about this as they continued to play—bits of church music, sailor songs, fairground dances, with Toni continuously decorating the music, as soon as he'd picked it up, in ways Alfredo himself would never have thought of. And he liked some things better than others, not necessarily because they were simpler; in fact rather the opposite. It depended on whether he found them interesting. So obviously there was nothing wrong with the music part of his mind. There must be some kind of kink, some blockage, somewhere else. If only . . .

"The tears of the salamander. Sovereign against all ills of body and mind."

No, he couldn't ask—in fact it would be a disaster. Uncle Giorgio hated his son. He wanted him dead. But . . . No, not yet. Wait until after Friday, when Uncle Giorgio was going to carry out some kind of test for the Second Great Work. Perhaps he'd know more then. There'd still be two days before Monday.

For the rest of the day every hour seemed to go slower than the one before. Alfredo took his *History of Rome* and the Latin dictionary down to supper, but could only pretend to read. Uncle Giorgio read in silence. Only as he rose at the end of the meal did he speak.

"Tomorrow, when we have breakfasted, you will sing the chant again to me. After that I will have preparations to make, so the rest of the day will be yours."

A

The chant went smoothly. Uncle Giorgio muttered briefly before they began and the Angels of Fire did not appear, though Alfredo could sense the faint prickling of their nearness. The words still meant nothing to him, but he now seemed to feel them all as separate things, each of them full of its own dark import. Neither they nor the music were strangers in his mouth.

"Well done," said Uncle Giorgio. "Now, as I told you, I have much to do. How will you spend your day?"

Alfredo had thought of going down to the town, hoping to find some friend to talk to, or at least a priest to whom he might confess his suspicions and terrors. But he guessed Uncle Giorgio wouldn't have allowed it, and besides, who would dare lift a finger against the Master of the Mountain?

"I thought I'd climb the mountain again," he said. "I'll ask Annetta for some food. I promise you I won't sing."

"Excellent. But do not go far beyond the shade of the woods, or tire yourself, or stay too long in the sun. Take one of the mules to ride. It would in any case be best if you were elsewhere today. I will also send Annetta and her idiot son away."

Alfredo hesitated, then seized his chance.

"They could come with me," he said. "I need Toni, really. I don't think I can manage a mule by myself."

"If you wish for such company. Send Annetta to me and I will give her instructions."

They climbed through the wood in silence, Toni leading the mule. Alfredo had wanted to dismount as soon as they were well away from the house, but Annetta had pushed him back into the saddle, shaking her head emphatically. She had been given her orders and she was going to obey them. It was still too early to eat by the time they came out of the trees, so they settled down for a rest, Annetta moving a little way off with Toni so as not to intrude on the gentry. It made no difference to her that Alfredo had come every evening to her kitchen and tempered her oven for her and chatted, nor that she had borne Uncle Giorgio a son. She was still, in her own mind, a servant, and knew her place, and did what she was told. Now Alfredo was going to try to persuade her not merely to disobey her master, but to help destroy him.

He watched them covertly. Toni was lying on his stomach, poking his finger into a tussock and peering with wonder at whatever it was he'd found there. Annetta was sitting bolt upright on a boulder, motionless, staring at nothing, her strong, proud face lined with the long endurance of grief. After a while Alfredo fetched his recorder from the saddlebag and started to play.

Annetta didn't stir, but Toni instantly looked up. Alfredo beckoned to him and he rose and scampered across, drawing his recorder from inside his smock as he came. Alfredo patted the rock beside him, and Toni sat and took up the tune. Annetta was staring at them now, her normally expressionless features filled with astonishment.

They played on. The mule fidgeted, swishing at flies. Crickets shrilled. Otherwise it seemed that not a leaf or blade was stirring. Alfredo could feel the presence of the mountain behind and beneath him, the whole vast, churning inward mass of it stilled for the moment by their playing. It wasn't something he was doing on his own—not even mainly his doing. It was the two of them together, here and for this short while come into their own, Masters of the Mountain.

Then Toni decided to switch to a tune that Alfredo had taught him and they'd played several times before. It was one of the rollicking airs that everyone used to dance to during the great Shrove Tuesday festival, waving their colored banners as they snaked in gaudy lines through the crowded streets. After a few bars Annetta rose, moved to a patch of ground where the slope eased almost level, raised her arms above her head and started to dance, twirling her skirt out and stamping to the rhythm of the tune. Alfredo almost stopped playing in amazement as she threw back her head and laughed with the joy of the dance. Her movements were quick, easy, definite, graceful. Every time she turned, her eyes came back to Toni. This was what life should be about, she seemed to be telling him, not drudgery, not fear, not power, not vengeance, but joy, the joy of being alive.

After a while Toni stopped playing, put his recorder down, rose and took a hesitant step toward her. Still dancing, she held out her hands to him. He walked across and took them and tried to copy the movements of her feet, clumsily at first, but then well enough for it to count as dancing. She linked arms with him and they whirled round each other, or she spun beneath his upstretched hand. Gradually Alfredo quickened the tune and they tried to keep pace, faster and faster, until they got into a tangle and collapsed and lay laughing and panting on the ground, while Alfredo applauded their performance and joined their laughter.

Before he'd even recovered his breath Toni came crawling back for his recorder, obviously ready to play on all day. He gave a disappointed shrug when Alfredo shook his head and rose, but then settled down and started to play softly to himself. Annetta was sitting up, watching him.

This looked like as good a moment as any. She rose as Alfredo crossed toward her and pointed at her son with a gesture of questioning wonder. Toni was already improvising his own variations on the tune they'd been dancing to.

"He's really good at it, isn't he?" said Alfredo. "Much better than I am. . . . Annetta, there's something I've got to talk to you about. . . . I think my uncle is planning to kill Toni."

She jerked with the shock and stood rigid, then gently nodded her head three or four times. She had been startled by his saying it but not by what he'd said. She raised her eyebrows.

"It's going to take a long time," he said. "Shall we have our lunch while I tell you?"

She fetched the saddlebag and opened the food she'd brought and laid it out on its wrappings, then settled opposite him. Toni joined them and ate with his usual intentness, but Alfredo did so in snatches, chewing while he put the next bit of his story in order. Annetta took only a few unnoticing mouthfuls.

He started right back at the beginning with his uncle's name-day gift, pulling it out from under his shirt and showing it to her. He left nothing out. Now for the first time he told her of the strange and wonderful moment when the Angel of Fire had appeared before Toni in the rose garden and affirmed his right to be numbered among the di Salas, and to inherit, when the time came, their long Mastership of the Mountain. He finished with his decision to talk to her now. The only things he left out were his own half-formulated plans.

"I'll know a bit more after tomorrow," he said, "when I've seen what happens in this test. And then with luck I'll know if I've got to try and fix it so that I can't help him on Monday—that's why I wanted those leaves you gave me. I don't think I can do anything unless I've got the mountain on my side—mine and Toni's—and the best way of doing that is to get the salamander back where it belongs. I don't know why—I just know. It's a bit like knowing when your fire's out of balance. But what I really want to know now is whether you'll let Toni help me. It's a risk, a terrible risk. If my uncle finds out . . . Look what he did to the *Bonaventura*."

She glanced at Toni, once again intent on his tussock, and then sat with her head bowed, rubbing one hand slowly over the back of the other. She straightened and nodded decisively. There were tears on her cheeks.

"Have you got a spare key to the furnace room?" he asked.

She shook her head.

"You mean there's just the one my uncle wears round his neck? Then we're going to have to break down the door. I can't do it alone—I'm not strong enough."

She shook her head decisively and made a that's-no-good gesture with her hands.

"You mean the door's too strong? Or there's something else—a spell or something?"

She nodded. That was bad news. Perhaps there was a way to undo a spell like that—he could ask the salamanders. But it might be one of the things they didn't know, like they didn't know what was going to happen. In which case . . . could he burn the door down somehow? There was probably a spell against that too. . . .

After a while he gave up trying to think of answers and went and fetched his recorder. Toni instantly leapt up and hurried over to join him. They spent the whole afternoon in the quiet shade, playing and resting and playing again, and only went back down through the wood when the sun began to move behind the mountain.

"Eat well," said Uncle Giorgio as they sat down to supper. "There will be no breakfast tomorrow. We fast until the rite is over. Come to my office as soon as you are dressed."

He seemed even edgier than he had that morning, and said nothing else throughout the meal. Nor did he read, but simply ate, silent and preoccupied, and left without another word. Alfredo had felt too nervous to eat much, but he dutifully filled his plate and then found he was hungry after his day on the mountain and polished it off without noticing. When he'd finished he went up to his room and sat in his window trying to read until it became too dark for that, then went to bed, but lay awake far into the night turning his problems uselessly over and over.

CHAPTER TWELVE

HE WOKE FEELING HAGGARD AND EXHAUSTED, dressed and went downstairs. Uncle Giorgio was in his study, and rose as Alfredo entered the room.

"One! Two! Three! Four!" shrieked the starling. It was answered by an angry chatter, and Alfredo saw that the brazier beneath its cage was gone and the other starling had now been brought down from upstairs and its cage was standing on the floor where the brazier had been. Uncle Giorgio ignored them both.

"Good," he said. "First we must robe."

He handed Alfredo a yellow garment stitched with red and green symbols. Alfredo put it on over his head and found that it reached almost to the floor. The sleeves were long too, with a tassel at the end. Uncle Giorgio's robe was an even more elaborate version of Alfredo's, and he wore a tall golden hat rising to a point and with a stiff upturned brim. Alfredo was bare-headed.

Uncle Giorgio picked up a crystal decanter and poured a little pale yellow liquid into two silver goblets. He spread his fingers over them, muttered briefly and handed one to Alfredo.

"Do as I do," he said. "What we are about to attempt is only a test, but involves mighty powers and must be performed with due solemnity. Now, first, three sips, and then three sips, and then three sips to finish the cup. Say the words after me. This is the First Purification. We begin."

He intoned a few syllables and waited for Alfredo to repeat them. The words were strange but sounded Persian, like those of the chant. A longer pause and he raised his goblet to his lips. Alfredo did the same. The liquid was intensely sweet in the mouth but fiery in the throat. Alfredo managed to judge his sips right and finished his goblet on the last one.

"Excellent," said Uncle Giorgio. "Bring the other bird and follow me."

Holding the cage high in front of him and moving as solemnly as a priest at Mass, he led the way along the corridor, round and down to the furnace room. He unlocked the door and locked it again behind him. The room had changed. The table beside the furnace where Uncle Giorgio kept his implements had been moved back to the wall, and some other objects had been shifted aside, leaving a clear space at whose center stood the brazier from upstairs. It was empty. Beneath it was a large tray spread with an even layer of fine sand, in which a single continuous groove had been scooped, making a five-pointed star enclosing the brazier. There was a lit lantern on a shelf beside the door.

Uncle Giorgio placed his cage on the lid of the furnace

and took the other one from Alfredo. He opened its door, reached in, caught the shrieking bird, withdrew it and handed the cage back to Alfredo, pointing to show him he was to put it down against the wall. By the time Alfredo turned back Uncle Giorgio was holding the bird in a grip that caused it to gape upward. He picked up a small dropper, dipped it into a bowl and squeezed a single drop of liquid into the bird's throat. He then put it into the cage on the furnace, caught and took out the first bird and did the same, and put it back in the cage with the other one. The two birds, which had screeched at each other almost continuously till this moment, fell silent. Uncle Giorgio picked up the cage and balanced it on the brazier, then took Alfredo by the shoulder, led him across to a point about three paces from the brazier and turned him to face it.

"Do not move from that spot and you will be quite safe," he said. "Watch me. When I raise my right hand, sing the chant. Here are your dark glasses. You will need them later."

Alfredo waited, his heart beating heavily with a mixture of wonder and terror, and the fierce excitement of being on the edge of strange knowledge. He watched Uncle Giorgio unstopper a large flask and very carefully, gripping the brazier for support and leaning out over the sand so as not to mark its surface in any other way, fill the star-shaped groove with glistening dark red granules. Finished, he restoppered the flask and stood back opposite Alfredo with the brazier exactly between them. He spread his arms wide, raised his head and began to speak.

Persian again, in a deep, strong voice, every syllable clear and exact. The room rang with the sound. It went on for a long while, but still the tension grew and grew. At last Uncle Giorgio fell silent. He drew his hands together before his mouth in a gesture of prayer. His lips were moving but the words were silent. He glanced at Alfredo, briefly raised his right hand and returned to his praying. Alfredo filled his lungs and sang.

He'd expected he might be too nervous to hit the first few notes, to have to steady himself into the chant, but the sound came strong and true. The air in the chamber prickled, and filled with a snowstorm of glowing flecks that swirled themselves into two tall fiery shapes, two Angels of Fire standing opposite each other one either side of the brazier, so that the four of them, two Angels and two humans, stood at the corner-points of a square. None of them stirred until the chant ended.

Then Uncle Giorgio spoke, two grating syllables. The Angels half-raised their arms. Fire streamed from their fingertips down toward the feet of the brazier. The pattern in the sand became a fiery star. Its flames were not red but an intense violet. They wavered as flames do, but did not spread and thicken. Instead they retained the precise outline of the star they sprang from, growing and growing until their tops bent inward and poured themselves into the bowl of the brazier beneath the cage and filled it.

The starlings showed no sign of being perturbed, but stood side by side on the single perch. One raised a foot and scratched under its chin. Then the flames shot up and enveloped the cage. There was no squawk from the birds, no sudden stench of burning feathers, only a faint odor, peppery but sweet, filling the chamber. The flames held the shape of the cage, increasing in intensity until Alfredo was forced to use his dark glasses. He could hear Uncle Giorgio's voice now, a steady mutter, the same dozen words over and over but becoming louder and louder as the light intensified. Despite the protection of his spectacles Alfredo could scarcely see Uncle Giorgio through the glare, but he made out a movement of some kind and at the same moment the Angels stretched out their arms toward the brazier, so Alfredo followed suit. At once he could feel the power being drawn from him, down his arms and out through his fingers. The light blazed stronger than the sun. He had to screw his eyes shut, despite the spectacles. Uncle Giorgio's voice was a harsh cry of triumph that suddenly snapped short. The light faded away and Alfredo could open his eyes.

Even without the spectacles he was blind. All he knew was that the Angels were gone.

"Stay where you are," said Uncle Giorgio. "It is not yet safe to move."

He started to pray again, different words, but again many times repeated with his voice dwindling away. Alfredo waited. Gradually his eyes adapted to the light of the single lamp. Now he could make out that there was only one bird on the perch. The other was lying on its side on the floor. He was unable to think about it. He felt extraordinarily tired and listless.

Uncle Giorgio's voice faded into silence. His lips stopped moving.

"It is over," he said in a weak and shaking voice. "Follow me. Bring the lantern."

He picked up the cage with the birds in it, unlocked the door and led the way out, locking the door behind them as before. He used the hand rope to haul himself up the stairs, and stopped to rest halfway. Alfredo's legs felt so weak that he could scarcely climb at all. It seemed a very long way back to the study. Uncle Giorgio hung the birdcage on its hook and fetched a different flask and two fresh goblets and poured some of the potion into each. While he waited Alfredo studied the birdcage. Yes, it was as he'd thought, but he hadn't been able to see clearly enough in the furnace chamber. The bird on the perch was the one from upstairs, the smaller one with the mottled breast. The one that could count was lying on the floor. It didn't stir. It seemed to be dead. Uncle Giorgio turned, and saw what he was looking at.

"Do not be alarmed," he said. "They are only birds. This was a test of my powers, not theirs. The older bird lacked the strength to receive what was given it. I do not. For me, perhaps, there is still some risk, but the prize is worth it. For you, none. The younger bird, as you see, is physically unharmed.

"Now the Second Purification. Copy me as you did before."

He handed Alfredo one of the goblets. They faced each other, intoning the words and sipping from the goblets. The warmth of the potion seeped through Alfredo's body, making him feel a little less feeble.

"Sit now, and rest," said Uncle Giorgio. "You are tired?"

"Yes, very."

"I too. All exercise of power takes strength. No, on second thought, go to your room and lie down. Annetta will bring you some food."

Alfredo staggered to his feet and left, closing the door behind him. But rising again so soon after sitting down seemed to have taken all strength out of him. He paused, leaning for a while against the wall to let his muscles recover. Behind him, through the door, he heard a scraping sound, and then the shriek of a starling. "One! Two! Three! Four!"

The final shock of understanding flooded his mind. It was like a sudden, fierce blow on the head, blanking out everything else. But for the wall he would have fallen to the ground. At last he pulled himself together and tiptoed away to his room.

⊢

He didn't go to bed, but sat in his favorite place in the window, sorting the whole thing through in his mind, fitting his new knowledge in with the old. By the time Annetta arrived with a tray of food he had it all pieced together, a single clear structure, a working machine with one terrible purpose.

"I've got something to tell you," he said. "Have you got time now? It's important."

She nodded and he told her what had happened that morning in the furnace room and the study, finishing with the cry of the starling.

152

"That was the young bird from his bedroom," he said. "I heard him pushing a crust into its cage, and it did what the old bird always did and counted up to four. It couldn't count before. Now it can. What he'd done, you see, was put the old bird's mind, its soul, what makes it *it,* into the young bird's body. That's what he's going to do on Monday—put himself into me. He ought to be dead, you see. The emanations from the furnace should have killed him long ago. He didn't know about that when he started. It's only the tears of the salamander that have been keeping him alive. But after Monday it won't matter because he'll have a new young body.

"That's why he's been so careful about me, seeing I had good food, shielding me from the furnace. And it's why he pretended to be ill when he took me to make his will. He didn't want people to be surprised when he died suddenly. And he wanted to make sure that Signor Pozzarelli was afraid of me, so he won't try and cheat him when he thinks he's only got this kid to deal with. And it's why he had to keep Toni around when really he hated him, in case he couldn't use me. There wasn't anyone else with the Mastership in his blood. But he didn't want to use him if he could possibly help it, in case what was wrong with Toni's brain meant that his own mind wouldn't work properly in it.

"And perhaps there's something wrong with Toni's seed, too, because he got it from my uncle—that's important, because he wants to have a son later on who's got the Mastership in his blood, so that when he's an old man again he can put himself into a new body again. That's how he's going to

153

live forever, you see. That's the Second Great Work. But now he won't need Toni anymore and he can get rid of him.

"Only I think we might be able to stop him. My uncle's told me how to get into the furnace room. He doesn't know that, but he has. But I'll need Toni for that. And you, too, for other things. All right?"

She didn't hesitate, but nodded firmly.

He told her his plan.

"I know it's dangerous," he said. "He's so much stronger than me. He's still Master of the Mountain. But we've got to try."

She thought grimly about it, sighed, and nodded again. She patted his shoulder encouragingly before she left. *It will be all right,* she was telling him. And *Thank you.*

When the day began to cool he took his recorder out to the rose garden. Before he reached the sunken garden he heard the sound of Toni's playing, a long, complicated phrase, repeated and repeated, but each time with small unexpected variations. For a while he stood and listened, astonished yet again by the ease and subtlety with which Toni performed. And all his own invention, utterly untaught. It was as if music was the air he breathed, and all he had to do was draw it into himself and breathe it out again as audible sounds, just as the salamanders did with their element of fire. And when Alfredo joined him and they played together there seemed to be no doubt in either of their minds who was the master and who the pupil.

Uncle Giorgio still looked tired at supper that evening and spoke little, but ate steadily and watched to see that Alfredo did the same. As he rose from the table he said, "Tomorrow I must again make preparations, and it would be better for you and Annetta and the idiot to be elsewhere. Do not climb the mountain again—that will overtire you."

"I could go out along to the rose garden and read. It's nice there, and there's some shade from the cypresses. Annetta could bring me some food."

"Good. But take some exercise. Walk in the woods a little to give yourself an appetite. Then on Sunday we will go to Mass and show ourselves to be good Christians, and to refresh ourselves. I am still tired and will need all my strength. And in the afternoon you and I together will begin the preliminaries to the rite, so that on Monday we are fully prepared."

"I'll do my best," said Alfredo.

"You are an excellent boy. Indeed, you are all that I had hoped."

As usual there were layers of meaning beneath the simple words, but now Alfredo understood what they might be.

He went to bed tense with expectation and hope and fear. Time had the feel of a river just before it reaches a weir. He could look back and see all that had happened laid out in order, full of swirls and crosscurrents and flurries. He could look forward, beyond the next couple of days, and see an unreadable tumult of foam. But between him and the lip of the weir the surface was almost smooth, tense, drawn silky taut by the pull of the coming drop.

Despite that, he fell asleep at last, slept heavily, and woke in broad daylight.

Downstairs he found that Uncle Giorgio had already breakfasted, but the tension had returned in full force, and he longed to be out of the house, so he ate nothing and left by the front door. He didn't immediately go out to the rose garden, but instead went northward into the old driveway, and stretched himself out once more on the lava flow.

He lay down and again molded his body to the night-chilled rock, imagining himself part of it, part of the mountain itself, letting his tension ease as that imagination became real, until he and the mountain were one thing, down to its white-hot roots, out to its farthest spurs and screes. The salamanders swam in his fiery veins, sang in his mind. It was a gift from the mountain. He guessed that even among the di Salas, only those whom the mountain had chosen could attain this understanding. You needed to give yourself to the mountain before it could return the gift. Perhaps, from the way Uncle Giorgio talked about the mountain and the salamanders, he had never himself achieved this, for all his skill and knowledge. He couldn't give himself. But another di Sala, long ago—whoever it was that had written the book from which the notes in the dictionary had been taken—must have lain like this on another outcrop, and so come to his understanding.

Yes, he thought. *Now I too understand. It all depends on the Master.*

There were two mountains. There was one as he had first known it, full of the fury of fire, dangerous, unpredictable in its rages, vengeful, hated and feared. That was Uncle Giorgio's mountain.

But if Alfredo's father had been Master . . . He also had a furious temper. He was a true di Sala. Anger was his birthright. It was in his blood. But his mountain would not have been like that. Those who lived below it would have understood its power, and seen perhaps its fury. But the fury would not have fallen on them. They would have thought of it not with dread, but with awe. Not with hatred, but with love.

Yes, sang the salamanders in his mind. *That is the mountain as it ought to be. That is our mountain.*

Now it was Alfredo's turn. He moved through the molten heart of the mountain and made himself known to the salamanders. Stilling their singing, they gathered round him. He sang to them in his mind, telling them everything he had seen and done and intended to do.

They answered with a burst of song, a complex polyphony of interwoven hopes and fears—eagerness to see their lost comrade freed, and the end of Uncle Giorgio's hated Mastership, dread of his powers and the vengeance he might take if Alfredo failed. And something else, a different kind of excitement. Alfredo understood what it was only when their singing changed itself and became the strange repeated phrase that Toni had been playing, effortlessly improvising, yesterday in the rose garden. New music, a new Master, a new world.

He listened for a while and then withdrew himself into his body, still lying on the lava flow out in the world of air.

There was somebody there—Toni of course, but this time sitting on the rock beside him, peacefully waiting.

"You heard?" he said. "You were there too? They can't help us, but they wish us well."

Toni nodded, apparently understanding. Together they went out to the rose garden.

A

Later Annetta came with food. She had questions to ask. It was a slow process, though she was very clever about it, gesturing expressively with her hands and nodding or shaking her head as Alfredo guessed his way to her meanings. How was he so sure Uncle Giorgio would go to Mass?

"He'll go if he possibly can. He's still tired after Friday, and he needs to get himself away from the mountain for a bit. And I think he probably wants to act old and sick in front of everyone, too. He won't worry about having to leave me behind, because the important thing for him is to get my body as strong as possible. The rest of me—my mind and so on—doesn't matter, and that's the bit the mountain wears out. I think he's *got* to go."

More gestures, more guessing.

"Yes, it's a risk. I think the mountain will be aware of it as soon as we start to move the salamander, but he won't notice as long as he's in the church—he can't feel the mountain there. As soon as he comes out he'll know something's happening, I'm fairly sure, but he won't know what. He'll feel it through the mountain and he'll want to hurry home. If he takes you with him—I hope he will—

anything you can do to slow him down a bit—make the mule go lame somehow, or give it some of those leaves while he's in church . . .

"And he may still have some magic way of getting up the mountain, quicker than riding. Just walking, he'll be going faster than us—our mules aren't going to like it, are they? But if everything goes all right we should be way up into the wood before he comes out of church. After that . . . I don't think we can possibly get to the top before he comes out of the wood, but provided we're a good way up the slope . . .

"And stay down there, Annetta. I think there's going to be an eruption. Don't come back till it's over. It's going to be very dangerous anywhere up on the mountain. . . ."

And so on, anxiously checking things through, over and over, Alfredo more and more tense, longing for the evening to be here, Annetta frowning with thought but patient and determined, and Toni sitting with his recorder, fetching his music endlessly out of nowhere, utterly untroubled. Eventually, rather than brood and think any more, Alfredo fetched his recorder and joined him. Slowly the tension eased as he filled his mind with listening to Toni and trying to follow where he led, and by the time Annetta laid out the food she had brought he realized he was hungry enough to eat. That, he thought, grimly amused, was just as well. He must have food in his stomach. To throw up.

The afternoon crept by. For a while he joined Toni, watching the comings and goings of ants round their nest, and experimented with dropping obstacles, or crumbs of bread, in the trails. They scrambled around in the woods, which were full of twisting little paths that Toni seemed to know. They returned to the rose garden and played their recorders. Toward evening Annetta gathered what she had brought into her basket, except for four plums. She gave two to Toni and two to Alfredo, making signs that they were to eat them. Then she went back to get supper ready, holding up a finger before she left to show that the other two should wait an hour and then follow.

The shadow of one of the cypresses lay across the dry pool. Alfredo placed a pebble on the rim, along into the sunlight. They left when the shadow touched the pebble.

He'd judged it wrong and they were a little too early. He checked the fire with extra care, not because it would make the slightest difference to how things went, but because it might be the last time he'd do it. Annetta handed him a mug and he drank the contents. He'd expected the potion to be dark and bitter, but it looked almost colorless in the gray mug and tasted slightly sweet on the tongue and then sharper at the back of his mouth. He went up to his room, by now so sick with nerves that he couldn't tell whether the drink was starting to do its work or not. When he went down to supper he found Uncle Giorgio already waiting for him. He looked even wearier than he had the evening before.

"You are rested?" he said. "I hope you have an excellent appetite."

"I don't know. I had a nice quiet day, but I don't feel very hungry."

"You must eat," snapped Uncle Giorgio.

There was a real sharpness under the words. *His* nerves

must be twanging too, Alfredo realized. Dutifully he put food on his plate, cut off a few small pieces, and started to chew and force his throat to swallow. The moment came like an eruption of the mountain. He flung back his chair, rushed to the window and vomited violently outside. The evening air filled with the vile stench of stomach stuff. When the spasms were past he stayed draped over the sill, shivering and sweating.

"What is this? You have been too long in the sun, you stupid child! What have you eaten?"

Uncle Giorgio's voice, close above his head, shook with fury. Alfredo pushed himself up from the sill.

"Nothing," he gasped. "Just what Annetta brought. It tasted fine. And I was careful about the sun. I wore my hat, but mostly I stayed in the shade. I really did."

"Go to your bed. Put the chamber pot beside you. Can you climb the stair?"

"I think so. . . . I think it's all gone, Uncle Giorgio. Out of me, whatever it was. I'll be all right for Monday, I promise. I will."

"That had better be the case. Very well. Go to your bed. I will come and see you later."

Alfredo forced his weak and trembling legs to carry him up the stairs and along to his room, where he took off his shoes, placed the chamber pot handy and clambered into bed fully clothed. Despite that, and the warmth of the evening, spasms of shivering shook him every minute or two. Soon Annetta arrived with a basket containing a couple of stone bottles, a flask and a small bundle wrapped in a cloth. When she slid the bottles in under the bedclothes beside him he discovered they were filled with hot water, almost too warm to touch with bare flesh but wonderfully comforting through his clothes.

"Thanks," he whispered. "That was worse than I expected. But I think it's all right. So far."

She put a finger to her lips, poured something from a jug she'd brought into a mug and placed it on the table beside him. Then she hid the bundle in the cupboard, put her finger to her lips again and left. The drink turned out to be lime water. He sipped a little and lay back.

A little later Uncle Giorgio arrived, still coldly angry but more in control of himself. He felt Alfredo's forehead, took his pulse and made him stick out his tongue.

"You have a headache?" he asked. "You see correctly, without spots or blurrings? You came here without falling."

"No. I mean my head's all right. And my eyes, I think. I felt a bit dizzy climbing the stairs, but it went. I'm better already, just weak and shivery."

"Tell me everything you have eaten today."

Alfredo did so, in detail. Uncle Giorgio nodded.

"The plums are the most likely cause," he said. "Some peasant with unclean hands may have touched them. So at least you ate them recently and the poison may not have worked into your system before you vomited it out. But if your bowels loosen in the night, eat nothing and drink all you can. I will see you in the morning before I go to Mass. You will stay here. Good night."

Alfredo lay where he was for a while, enjoying the warmth of the stone bottles. The shiverings grew less, and ceased. By nightfall he felt fine, but ravenously hungry. As the last light faded he heard a soft footfall in the corridor outside, so he closed his eyes, slowed his breathing down and lay still. The door creaked gently. The footsteps crossed the room. A bony hand touched his forehead. He didn't stir or change his breathing until the door had closed again and the footsteps dwindled along the corridor.

Still he waited, but at last rose, went to the cupboard, found Annetta's bundle by touch and carried it to the window, where he opened it on the window seat, spreading the cloth round it. She'd provided a simple meal, slices of bread and soft cheese. He ate, crouching low over the cloth in case scattered crumbs might betray them when Uncle Giorgio came in the morning. When he'd had enough he carefully wrapped the bundle and put it back in the cupboard. He hadn't discussed any of this with Annetta—it had all been her idea. So had the plums. If anything went wrong it wouldn't be her fault.

He undressed, went back to bed and fell almost instantly asleep. It was as if, along with his stomach stuff, he had vomited out all the day's anxieties and forebodings. He didn't wake until Annetta opened the door in the morning, well past sunrise.

CHAPTER THIRTEEN

ANNETTA PUT DOWN THE TRAY SHE WAS CARRY-
ing, made signs to him to stay where he was and put her
finger to her lips, then helped him sit up, stuffed an extra
pillow behind him and laid the tray across his knees. There
wasn't much on it, just a bowl of thin broth and a single
slice of bread. Alfredo was still hungry, but he spun it out,
sipping the broth and nibbling the bread, and was only just
finishing as Uncle Giorgio arrived.

"Well, I trust you feel better," he snapped. "You slept
well?"

"Yes, thank you, Uncle Giorgio. I feel almost all right.
Just a bit feeble. And, er, empty."

"No more vomiting? No looseness of the bowels?"

"I don't think so. I haven't tried yet. There isn't, er . . ."

"No doubt. Toni, apparently, has the same sickness, so it
will have been the plums that caused it. In an hour's time
you may eat a little more, and again an hour after that. If
any sign of the sickness returns, do not eat. Annetta will
leave food for you in the breakfast room. Eat nothing else.
You understand?"

"Yes, of course. . . . Can I get up?"

"Yes, but stay in the house, out of the sun. I will see you on my return from Mass."

He marched out of the room without another word. Alfredo rose, washed and dressed, then finished the remains of last night's supper, listening intently all the time for the sound of footsteps in the corridor. After that there was nothing to do but wait in his window until Uncle Giorgio left.

All his anxieties came crowding back. His plan was like a chain, each link depending on the one before it. If one link snapped, the plan would fail. What then? Run away, as he had told Annetta? How? Where to? Who on the island would risk the fury of the Master of the Mountain? He tried to force himself to think about the problem, but his mind kept slithering back to the chain, testing it through, link after link after link. And again. And again.

At last Uncle Giorgio appeared from behind the house, already riding his mule, with Annetta striding at his side. Just as he rounded the terrace he turned and looked up at the house. Alfredo waved. Uncle Giorgio raised his hand in brief acknowledgment and headed down the hill. Still Alfredo waited until they had long disappeared among the olive trees, then hurried downstairs.

He found Toni sitting placidly in the kitchen. There was a satchel on the table beside him, which he pushed toward Alfredo with a smile. Alfredo glanced inside. More food.

"Your mother is a marvelous woman," he told Toni. Toni smiled, but there was no knowing whether he understood the words, or only the tone. Alfredo beckoned to him and led the way out into the yard.

Together they fetched out the two remaining mules and tethered them to separate rings in the stable wall. They gave them nose bags to keep them quiet, and then brought out the two harnesses and the cradle to carry the salamander's bucket. Alfredo worked out how it assembled and then stood for a while checking round the yard, making as sure as he could that this stage of the plan would really work. The main problem was going to be the weight of the salamander's bucket, filled with some of the molten mass from the furnace. Strong though Toni was, Alfredo didn't believe that the two of them could carry it up from the cellars between them, and then lift it into the cradle between the mules. That's why the second bucket had been so important.

There was nothing more he could think of. He sighed with anxiety and led the way back into the kitchen. The clock said it was still twenty minutes to go before the start of Mass, so he opened the satchel and forced himself to eat. Toni had no such problems.

With five minutes to go he repacked the satchel, took it out and stowed it in one of the saddlebags, went back to the kitchen, lit a lantern with a spill from the fire and led the way down to the cellar. Toni gazed without interest at the massive door of the furnace chamber, and turned inquiringly to Alfredo. Now came the first true test, the first link in the plan. If this succeeded, there would be no going back. If it failed . . .

Alfredo put the lantern on the floor, aligned his hands in front of his mouth and moved his fingers over the stops of an imaginary recorder. Toni took his real one from under his smock and put it to his lips. Quietly Alfredo began to sing the old Persian chant of summoning. After the first two notes Toni joined smoothly in.

And an Angel of Fire was there, with them, filling the height and width of the gloomy passage with its blazing presence. Alfredo almost lost the chant, stunned by the sudden nearness of such power, so much stronger, more vivid, than that of the two that Uncle Giorgio had summoned to his rite with the starlings. Now he understood what the notes had meant when they had talked about the difference between the Greater and Lesser Angels. Those two had been of the sort that could be commanded by a man with the Knowledge. But this was indeed one of the Greater Angels—perhaps the same one that had appeared before Toni in the rose garden. They could ask it, but it would choose whether to do what they asked.

The Angel waited, impassive, until the chant ended, and even then seemed to ignore Alfredo. Instead it faced Toni directly, bowed its head and waited again. Toni looked to Alfredo for guidance, and now at last the Angel turned to him. He, too, bowed his head as the Angel had done, placed his finger onto the keyhole of the lock, and spoke the two grating syllables with which Uncle Giorgio had commanded the Lesser Angels to light the star around the brazier. He stood back and watched the Angel reach out an arm and place its hand over the lock. A white light gathered itself inside the Angel's body, pulsed gently down its arm and settled in a dome of pure heat over the lock. The passage filled with smoke and the stench of burnt timber. The Angel withdrew its arm, turned and bowed to Toni, and vanished.

Alfredo pushed on the door and it swung open. There was a pool of molten iron on the step below the lock.

Toni seemed dazed by this second encounter with the Angel. Alfredo had to take him by the elbow and lead him into the furnace chamber, where he stood, slowly gazing round with unseeing eyes while Alfredo fetched the things they would need from the stack in the corner: the two buckets with their carrying pole, the ladle and the tongs. He fetched both pairs of dark glasses from the shelf and fitted Uncle Giorgio's onto Toni for him. He didn't bother with the lead screen—they would be moving around too much. They would have to take their chance with the emanations.

Now, at last, he raised the lid of the furnace.

There was no sign of the salamander, so he took the lid off the smaller bucket and began to ladle the molten liquid into it. With its bowl barely half full the ladle became almost too heavy for him to control. He stopped when he could no longer lift the bucket by himself.

He closed the furnace, put the lid on the bucket and fastened its clasp. The metal of the bucket itself was already too hot to touch. This was something he hadn't thought of, but for the moment it didn't matter. He went over to Toni and removed his dark glasses. Toni seemed to have woken at the change from the glare of the furnace to the dim light of the lantern and was now looking round the chamber in an interested way, as though seeing it for the first time. Alfredo led him to where he wanted him, fetched the carrying pole and slid the hook in under the handle of the bucket.

"Ready?" he said. "You take that end."

He grasped his end of the pole and lifted it a few inches, waited till Toni had copied him, stood upright and led the way out into the passage. The load was heavy but manageable. They took the stairs slowly, with the bucket swinging uncomfortably to and fro as they climbed. Already Alfredo could feel the heat beaming out from it. Once up they could hurry along the corridors and out through the kitchen into the yard. He settled the bucket down by the stable wall, close to the mounting block, unhooked the pole and went back with Toni to the furnace chamber.

This time, the moment he opened the lid the salamander rose from beneath the surface. Alfredo was expecting it to look at him and he would then sing *Levavi oculos* — *I will lift up mine eyes unto the hills* — while he told it through the music what was happening. Instead it stared for a moment at Toni, opened its small round mouth and, unprompted, started to sing. Toni took out his recorder and joined it. The salamander's song was a strange mixture of wild joy and deep grief, joy at the coming of a new and kindly Master, grief for him, for what he was. The salamander wept.

On an impulse Alfredo picked up Uncle Giorgio's little ladle and leaned forward to harvest the salamander's tears. He remembered something that one of the priests in the cathedral had told them, explaining some miracle of healing: "The mind is spirit, but the brain is flesh. A madman has an ailment of the mind, and therefore of spirit. An idiot has one of the brain, and therefore of the flesh."

Sovereign against all ills of the flesh, he thought.

The song finished and the salamander disappeared beneath the surface. Alfredo tipped the contents of the ladle into the phial, but had to wake Toni from his half-trance before he could give it to him.

"Drink it," said Alfredo, miming the action. Toni obeyed and gave the phial back. Alfredo hadn't expected anything much to happen. When Uncle Giorgio, on the verge of death, had drunk the tears it had been some while before they had had any effect. And time was pressing. He picked up the ladle and filled the remaining bucket with as much as he thought they could lift, then picked up the tongs, held them over the furnace and softly began *Levavi oculos* at last.

The salamander rose and at once reached for the tongs, scrambled up and let Alfredo close them gently on it. It peeped pitifully as he lifted it out and across, and huddled down into the molten heat in the bucket, though it could barely get its whole body beneath the surface. In that brief transfer Alfredo had seen that the salamander was exactly like the pendant he wore round his neck, right down to the hooked barb at the end of its tail.

He was about to close the lid of the bucket when Toni stopped him with a grunt, and then, to Alfredo's astonishment, picked up the ladle and added another bowlful of the liquid to the bucket. He tested the weight, and only then allowed Alfredo to close and fasten the lid.

As he did so Alfredo noticed that heat was now radiating from its surface in a way it hadn't done before, and there was a slight roiling motion as if the liquid were slowly coming to a boil. He guessed that this must be something to do with the salamander's having left it. When he turned he found that Toni had already hooked the carrying pole into the handle of the bucket and was standing ready, but holding the pole some way in from its end, so that he would be taking a larger share of the weight. They left the door of the chamber open and the lantern still burning.

Out in the yard they heaved the bucket up onto the mounting block, fetched the mules, tethered them to rings on either side of the block, slid the poles of the cradle into their harness, and then stationed them so that the central ring of the cradle was close beside the block. Now . . .

But it wasn't going to work. In Alfredo's plan he was simply going to heave the bucket across into its place in the cradle while Toni held the mules steady, but now, faced with the task, he realized it was beyond his strength.

"It's more than I can manage," he said, and scrambled off the block, but before he could start back across the yard for the spare bucket and the ladle Toni grunted and stopped him, laying his hand on Alfredo's arm and tapping himself on the chest. He seemed utterly confident.

"All right," said Alfredo, taking the bridle. "But watch out. The bucket's going to be hot. You'll need a bit of sacking or something."

Gingerly Toni tested the bucket, frowned slightly and climbed the block. He tested the handle again, this time more firmly, positioned himself, grasped the handle and with a single flowing movement swung it across into the cradle ring. He rose, blowing on his palms, and grinned at Alfredo. Yes, the bucket was hot, but nothing like as hot as Alfredo, or Toni himself, apparently, had expected.

Nothing like as hot as the other one either, it turned out. That was now beaming out heat like the open door of an oven. They used the carrying pole to take it across to the block.

"We can't pour it in," said Alfredo. "It would be far too dangerous. I'll go and get the ladle. You see if you can find a way of getting the lid off. Don't burn yourself. It must be something the salamander's doing, keeping the other one cool. It did it in the furnace too."

He raced off, checking on his way through the kitchen how much time had gone. More than he'd thought. In twenty minutes Mass would be over. As soon as Uncle Giorgio stepped out of the church he'd know that something was happening up on the mountain, and the closer he came to home the more he would feel it and the faster he'd hurry.

It was warm now in the furnace room. More than warm. The furnace was beaming out heat, much like the bucket in the yard. Alfredo snatched up the ladle and raced back. He found Toni crouched over the bucket, his face streaming with sweat while he levered at the clasp with a hoof pick and a screwdriver. Alfredo took the lead mule's bridle again and watched Toni anxiously, getting his breath back. If Toni didn't succeed in the next few minutes they'd have to give up, and the salamander must take its chance with what was already in the bucket. . . .

There was a sudden click. Toni rose and backed away, gasping. He unfastened the clasps on the bucket in the cradle with his bare hands and then used a leather apron he'd found to lift the lid of the other bucket clear. The salamander was again making its peeping complaint, but stopped as Toni ladled the hot liquid in for it, then tipped in what was left in the other bucket and closed and clasped the lid of the one in the cradle. He then calmly began to fold the apron, as if they had all the time in the world.

"We're in a hurry now," said Alfredo. "He'll be coming out of the church in ten minutes. We've got to get as far up the mountain as we can before he reaches the top of the wood."

Alfredo nodded, but finished folding the apron and tucked it into the harness. With the same assurance he gestured to Alfredo to switch to the rear mule. The change in him was astonishing. He now seemed to understand everything that was said to him, and all that was happening, and why, and to be fully aware of the urgency, but at the same time to be completely untroubled, without any of Alfredo's twanging tensions and anxieties. Nor was there any doubt who was in command. Now, for a while, the mountain had two real Masters, Toni and Uncle Giorgio, and the coming contest would be between them, with Alfredo merely helping Toni as best he could. He accepted the change with relief.

They untied the halters and started up the hill. Uncle Giorgio's mules were well mannered, as mules go, and used to the mountain, but the cradle was an awkward burden on the steep and twisting track, so they toiled slowly up through the wood, Alfredo with all his inner senses tense for the moment when he would first feel the outburst of Uncle Giorgio's fury on discovering how he had been betrayed. That would be no merely human rage, he was certain. It would be the rage of the Master, an eruption like that of the mountain. Even here, far up the slope, he was sure to sense it.

By the time they reached the top of the wood he was almost exhausted. Last evening's loss of food was taking its toll. What he had eaten since wasn't enough to replace it. His calves and thighs seemed emptied of muscle, barely able to heave him another step upward. His lungs gasped uselessly at the dry, hot air. In the trees' last shade they halted briefly to drink from the water bottles and cram food into their pockets.

"He must be almost at the house by now," said Alfredo.

Toni nodded and turned to gaze at the slope above them. He shook his head and beckoned Alfredo forward, then pointed up the slope and offered him the bridle of the lead mule, spreading his hands in a gesture of bafflement. His meaning was obvious. Not enough people climbed the mountain to leave a clear continuous track on the stony surface, and he had never done so.

Alfredo had, though only once. He studied the slope and spotted a jut of rock a few hundred paces farther up. That was the crag he had noticed when he and Uncle Giorgio had been making their way down from the crater, because it felt like one of the places where some of the powers of the mountain seemed to run close to the surface and might be summoned forth and used. He pulled his hat from behind his back and fitted it onto his head, then led the way on into the full weight of the sun.

Hardly had they started to climb again when the explosion came. It swept up through the still, hot noon with the onset of a sudden squall. The air seemed to crackle with it. The mountain quivered at its touch. Alfredo staggered. Toni, behind him, cried aloud. Both of them had felt it, and knew what it meant. Uncle Giorgio had reached the furnace chamber and seen the lock melted and the salamander gone. Now it was a question of how fast he could follow. Alfredo attempted to quicken his pace but his legs refused to respond. He huddled into himself, contracted his whole being into the effort to drive himself on, his eyes intent on the next step ahead, only glancing up now and then to check how far it still was to the landmark crag.

They weren't going to make it, nothing like. His muscles had nothing left to give. His whole body seemed to be on fire with the effort. The world was on fire, a roaring, red haze. There were voices in the roaring, one voice deeper, almost, than sound itself. The voice of the mountain, calling him. He surrendered himself to the voice, to the fire, to the mountain, letting it flood his body with its power, drive his limbs on and up in paces that were suddenly light and easy, like the dance of flames.

He looked up. The whole mountainside was pulsing with flame, flame from the spirit world, the world of the Angels of Fire, invisible except to eyes that could see through the sense of fire. Beside him the mule plodded on unnoticing, seeing only the everyday mountainside. Alfredo saw it rippling with the colors of sunset, like a monstrous ember, and the crag he was aiming for not as a darker jut of rock, but as a white-hot focus of the mountain's power, bright as the sun-stuff in the salamander's furnace.

The crag came closer and closer, but all the time, from behind him, he could sense the onrush of the Master's rage, rapidly gaining on them, sweeping up the hill, faster than any human, any mule or horse, could climb. Just as they reached the crag Toni gave a shout of warning. Alfredo switched hands on the bridle, turned and looked back. The fire vision cleared from his eyes. For a moment there was nothing to be seen, and then the Master burst out from among the trees.

He came in the form of a compact rolling cloud, denser and darker than the thickest smoke and full of orange lightnings. Alfredo's stomach shrank inside him. How could he ever have imagined he could face this *thing*? And he was nowhere near where he had wanted to be, high up the slope, close to the heart of the mountain and its inmost fires, before the struggle began. But his only hope was still to stick to his plan. The crag was at least a place from which some of the powers of the mountain could be drawn. Uncle Giorgio had no such advantage. He let go of the bridle, turned aside, and put his back to the rock. The mountain spoke to him through it.

Yes, here! it said.

He squared his shoulders, raised his head, filled his lungs and sang.

"Let God arise, and let his enemies be scattered. Let them also that hate him flee before him. Like as the smoke vanisheth, so shalt thou drive them away. And like as wax melteth at the fire, so shall the ungodly perish at the presence of God."

Inwardly the mountain stirred. Something inside Alfredo came alive at the words, his own birthright of rage and the desire for vengeance as he had first become aware of them, lying on the old lava flow across the driveway and listening to the far voices of the salamanders telling him what his uncle had done. He gathered that anger into a compact and burning force and drove it down toward the thing on the slope.

The thing halted. It changed shape, grew a head, arms, legs, human in form, but monstrous. Monstrous in its size, in its horror, in its power. It raised its arms in front of it, and power streamed out of them, visible, implacable, a rolling wave of the same dark smoke-stuff advancing steadily up the slope, its wings moving faster than the center, curving forward into an arc, ready to close round Alfredo, deceiver and betrayer of the Master, and engulf him. Where was Toni? Why wasn't he helping? Dimly he remembered seeing him climb on past the mules as he had turned to face the Master.

He called the powers of the mountain back, focussed them through himself and beamed them against the wave. It halted, swirled into a vortex, a whirlpool of smoke-stuff that simply sucked them in and made them part of itself. Then it came on.

His resolve, his awareness of his own power, wavered. He sensed another power nearby, above him. He glanced up. Toni was there, on the lip of the crag, facing the coming wave, his recorder ready at his lips.

It wasn't enough. Nothing was enough. Desperately he sang on.

"O God, when thou wentest forth before the people, when thou wentest through the wilderness, the earth shook and the heavens dropped. . . ."

High and fierce, the notes of the recorder threaded the human voice.

Now the mountain answered. Below, behind and above him Alfredo felt the surge of its anger. There was a deafening groan. The whole slope heaved like the deck of a ship in a storm. The mules, which had been waiting patiently just below him, apparently oblivious to the struggle, lost their footing. The hind one fell, dragging the other down and its harness free of the cradle, then struggling to its feet and bolting away along the slope. The lead mule rose and reared, squealing. The cauldron was tossed out and came slamming down onto a boulder. The lid flew off and the contents spilled down the slope, with the salamander floundering helplessly in the sun-stuff. It raised its head and gave a piercing scream, a note of pure agony. As if at the sound, the mountain tore itself apart.

The rent opened almost at Alfredo's feet, releasing a blast of sulphurous heat, forcing him back. The salamander shrieked again. He glanced down the slope and saw that the cloud was now barely twenty paces below the crag. He could see nothing beyond. In a few heartbeats it would all be over. But there was still time for one part of his revenge. The leather apron that Toni had used to handle the bucket had fallen out of the harness as the mules had bolted. He ran, snatched it up and darted across to the salamander. Its golden body, exposed to the naked air, was now streaked with black. It was dying like a dying coal as the heat faded from it, while it desperately tried to drag itself toward the fiery crack that had opened in the mountainside. Alfredo wrapped the apron round his hands, snatched the salamander up, darted back as close as he could get for the heat, and tossed it into the chasm. His hair and eyebrows were scorched before he turned away.

He realized that he had stopped singing. It didn't matter. In this one thing, at least, he had defeated the man who had murdered his family. Calmly he turned to see how much time was left him before the end. The cloud seemed to have halted, to have lost some of its menace—yes, surely, to be thinning. From the top of the crag, strong and true above the immense rumblings of the mountain, came the sound of Toni's recorder. It was hard to believe he could draw such sounds, so piercingly fierce and loud, from a simple wooden pipe. What he was playing was no longer the music of the psalm; it was something Alfredo had never heard before, something that seemed to come into Toni's mouth and fingers in the very moment of playing, but this time not out of the air. He was drawing it forth from the mountain, the music of anger and of fire, and breathing it out through his recorder so that it filled the whole hillside.

Wearily Alfredo climbed up the slope and round onto the crag and stood beside him. From here they could see out over the remains of the cloud and all the way down the slope.

The Master still stood where they had last seen him, unflinching in his monstrous shape, as he fought to exert his power over the mountain. For the moment he seemed to have succeeded. The rent in the hillside ran halfway down from the crag to where he stood, narrower at its lower end than where it had started. There he was holding it, while Toni strove to drive it on. Alfredo waited for the note and joined the contest.

"Let God arise, and let his enemies be scattered...."

At the first phrase of the fire psalm, deep below their feet, the host of the salamanders wove their shrill voices into the music. The mountain regathered its strength. Again the hillside heaved. A huge explosion drowned all other sounds. Roasting gases burst out of the gulf, tossing red-hot rocks far into the air, and a great wave of churning lava boiled out and flooded down the slope.

The Master doubled his size and flung his power against it. The onrush paused. Toni's music changed and became a rapid pattern of intricate shrill notes. A twisting rope of fire coiled itself out of the gulf, floated down toward the sorcerer, and began to curl around him. At the moment it completed the circle he lost his magical shape and became Uncle Giorgio. Released from his hold, the mountain rent itself open all the way down to the trees. The chasm forked, its two arms passing either side of Uncle Giorgio. The rope tightened and snatched him into the flaming gulf.

They stood gasping, stunned, staring dazedly at the huge outflow of lava welling from the rent and flooding down the mountain. Alfredo felt utterly empty, spent. Already exhausted from the climb, he'd now poured out inner strengths, strengths he'd never known were there, in the struggle against the Master. Toni, too, was haggard with the effort, stoop-shouldered and trembling. His face was gray and trenched with deep lines. The likeness was very clear. He was Uncle Giorgio's son. He had just killed his own father.

Toni recovered first, turning to Alfredo with a worried

frown and gesturing at the tide of lava, and then pointing up and over the wood and down to the town below.

There are people down there. My mother, perhaps.

With an effort Alfredo pulled himself together. Behind and below him he could feel the rage of the mountain, unappeased by Uncle Giorgio's death. Masterless now, it was angry of its own nature, filled with the anger of fire, purposeless, pure and huge, and at last allowed to burst out after so long lying in chains. *Burn and destroy!* it bellowed in its thunders. *Burn and destroy!* The madness of fire. How easily an evil-minded Master could harness that anger to his own ends.

Yes, and he had felt it before, that selfsame madness brought across the sea to a northern city and deliberately focussed onto a loving home through the burning glass of Uncle Giorgio's vengefulness and greed for power. And then again, onto the *Bonaventura*. And once more, though this time unchannelled, when he and Uncle Giorgio had stood on the rim of the crater, and he had inadvertently woken the wrath of the mountain by singing the fire psalm to it, and it had taken their combined strengths to force it back into its prison.

There was no hope of doing that now. He had no such strength left, nor did Toni. Somehow, that anger must be appeased. Another memory came to him—waiting with Mother in the square in front of the cathedral while Father argued with a fellow baker and his brother Giorgio larked with his cronies, and quietly, for the mere joy of it, singing to himself the music he had just been listening to in the cathedral. That had been the moment that had changed everything, that had set him on the course to the place where he now stood. The gift of the salamanders.

It was as if everything that had happened from that moment to this was part of a single purpose. He turned, raised his arms toward the summit of the mountain and sang.

"Lord, now lettest thou thy servant depart in peace, according to thy word. . . ."

The notes of the descant rose like lark song through the bass thunderings of the mountain. Toni's recorder joined quietly in, swooping and soaring around the line. And now more music, sweeter and higher than either, as from the unimaginable heat of the gulf below the salamanders raised their voices in exultation at the return of their lost comrade, and the fall of the hated Master, and the new beginning, the different kind of Mastership that his heir would bring.

The mountain paused as if to listen. It groaned, shuddered, and groaned again, and at last, as Alfredo and the salamanders fell silent and the quiet notes of Toni's recorder faded into the afternoon air, was still.

At the bidding of the salamanders the mountain had acknowledged its new Master.

They stared at each other, shaking their heads in disbelief. The lava was still welling out of the chasm below them, but moving more slowly and in less of a flood. In the pauses between its rumblings they could hear the voices of the alarmed rooks as they circled above the trees, and from far below that the clank of a cracked church bell calling the people to evensong.

Toni pointed over Alfredo's shoulder. He turned and saw that up the slope, well to their left, the lead mule was wrestling to free itself from something that had trapped it. They trudged and clambered across to it. Somehow a length of chain, trailing from the cradle, had caught under a boulder, and the panicking mule, struggling to wrest it free, had only jammed it faster. Toni grasped the bridle and murmured to the mule and stroked its ears and teased it under its jaws while Alfredo unhitched the chain and released the cradle from the harness. The mule's panic ebbed away and it stood utterly exhausted, with its head bowed almost to the ground, shuddering, covered with foam, its lungs heaving, while Alfredo removed what remained of its harness.

One saddlebag was still there, with some of the food left in it. They settled on the slope and ate in silence, looking out over the strait. The steady beat of the church bell floated up from the town.

"Right at the end," said Alfredo, "that burning rope—you did that?"

Toni nodded.

"How did you know?"

For answer Toni leaned across and touched Alfredo's smock, just at the point where the salamander pendant hung against his chest on the chest. As far as Alfredo knew, he had never seen it, but now he knew it was there. Alfredo wasn't surprised.

"The salamanders?" he said. "They told you?"

Toni nodded again, and then raised a warning finger as the tolling changed and became a wild rhythmless clangor, joined now by several other bells, sounding the alarm, telling the townspeople that the mountain had woken.

"They've taken their time," said Alfredo, and then, "No, I suppose it hasn't been that long. It just seemed like it. Well, it's over now. I think we can hold it."

But Toni was frowning, and gazing not down toward the town where the sounds came from, but more to the right. Yes, Alfredo could feel it too. Something was happening, something with fire in it, halfway up the hill, about where the Casa di Sala must be . . .

. . . and then, from that point, a burst of light, brilliant even in the bright sunshine. With it one dense ferocious impulse, a blast of pure power, not coming from the mountain but bursting from a single center with huge, astounding force. Light-dazzled, stunned, they saw only dimly the blast-wave traveling up the hill, tossing the treetops about as if in a hurricane. The sound of the explosion reached them first, a long, immense, roaring bellow. Before it ended, the blast, an almost solid wave of roasting air, knocked them flat.

Alfredo pushed himself groaningly up out of the darkness and stared down the hill. Half the trees in the wood seemed to be down. Several fires had started. Beyond that stood an uprushing column of dark smoke, rising and rising, which at its top widened into a pale, churning cloud like a child's drawing of a tree. In only one way was it like the fire of the mountain: It was filled with the same rage.

Toni was already on his feet, staring. He raised both arms high and gave a great wordless shout, a call, a summons.

At the sound the air became full of the Angels of Fire, as

usual almost invisible in the afternoon sunlight, but still blazingly there. They hovered, waiting for Toni. He called again and swept his arms down and outward. *Remove,* he told them. They turned and streamed away toward the strange, still rising cloud until they hovered in a ring around its top. Nets of fire fell from each of them, joined themselves, narrowed in a fiery mesh around the column, bright against its blackness all the way down to the ground. The Angels rose again, picking up cloud and column and, at its base, the sun-bright ball of heat from which it sprang, and bore the whole thing up and away toward the sun.

Alfredo watched the burning mass dwindle to a spark and vanish.

"Well done!" he whispered, stammering with wonder. "How did you . . . What . . . ? Oh, I think I know. That was the salamander's furnace. As long as it had the salamander in it . . . But it started to change as soon as we took the salamander out, and last time I went it was too hot to get near."

Toni nodded. That was something he'd already known— not guessed, as Alfredo had—just as he had understood the menace of the cloud and known how to overcome it. That knowledge and that power were part of his inheritance. He was now truly Master of the Mountain, come into his birthright. His whole stance expressed his Mastership as he stood gazing down the slope and out over the strait. But then, with a sudden, urgent movement he turned to Alfredo. His whole face was full of questioning worry. His mouth struggled to shape a word.

"Annetta? Your mother?" said Alfredo. "I told her not

to follow Uncle Giorgio back, to find somewhere safe, in case there's an eruption. She told me where, and I said we'd go and look for her there."

Toni nodded doubtfully, but settled down beside Alfredo to finish their meal. The mule had bolted again, but was too tired to go far and was standing a little way off, braying pitifully for its companion. The town bells still clamored their alarm. Dazedly Alfredo began to wonder what he should do now, how much he dared tell anyone. He glanced up when Toni gave a grunt and rose. The second mule was shambling back across the hillside. The first one staggered to meet it.

"I suppose we'd better go and tell people it's all over," said Alfredo.

As he scrambled down toward the mules, it struck him that perhaps he now knew why the two brothers had quarrelled. Uncle Giorgio needed two people to manage the mules, and so had tricked Father into helping him, and when Father had realized what was really happening he'd tried to stop it. Those were the two angry voices the salamander had heard. So it was up here, on this mountainside, that the terrible rift between them had opened, loosing the raging fires between them.

Well, maybe. He would ask the salamanders about it sometime.

The mules seemed relieved to be caught but it took a while to coax them close enough to the lava flow to make a start down the path, scrambling every so often round or over tangles of fallen branches. The flow had now ceased moving, but there were places where the twists of the path took them too close to stand the heat and they had to pick their way down through the trees. The sun was setting by the time they came out onto the old driveway and made their way home along it.

But Casa di Sala was gone. The lava had reached it, buried it and then piled itself up on the terrace below and there finally solidified. There was no sign of the explosion in the furnace room, so that must have happened just before the lava covered everything. Nothing was left. The mountain had made it all part of itself.

They gazed at it for a while and then, without a word, headed on downhill. Alfredo found he was thinking more coherently. What next? Take the mules to the inn. Find Annetta, if possible. Then Signor Pozzarelli. Tell him just enough of the truth to make him understand that the mountain still had a Master. . . .

As it turned out, Annetta found them, climbing up toward them through the dusk, leading the third mule. Toni ran to meet her, and she flung her arms round him and hugged him, sobbing with relief. After a while he took her by the shoulders and gently pushed her away from him and stood erect, gazing down into her face. His mouth worked. The syllables when they came were slow and grating, like the hinges of a long-closed door, but the word was unmistakable.

"Mama."

Her face turned white under its tan. Her mouth fell open. She stared at Toni, who simply stood there, smiling and confident. She turned to Alfredo.

"The tears of the salamander," he said. "My uncle could

have done it long ago. He was a horrible man. He killed my family and my friends on the *Bonaventura*. He was going to steal my body from me. But what he did to Toni—I think it's worse than anything. His own son!

"Casa di Sala is gone, Annetta. All gone. The mountain's buried it. We're going on down."

It was dusk when they reached the town. It was still in an uproar, windows smashed in by the blast from the furnace, roofs stripped of their tiles, bells stopping and starting, people standing in the streets guarding piles of their precious possessions, ready to flee, others dragging loads toward the harbor in the hope of finding space on some boat, yet others just standing around exchanging rumors. At the inn Annetta made as if to stay with the mules, but Alfredo said, "No. You've got to come too."

One tower of the church had fallen. The square in front was crowded, groups of people standing waiting for news, others hurrying on errands, others on their knees praying. Alfredo pushed and wriggled his way through and up the steps to Signor Pozzarelli's door and banged the knocker.

"You'll get a flea in your ear, sonny," somebody called. "Doesn't know any more than anyone else."

And indeed the door was opened by Signor Pozzarelli himself, his face red with anger, his mouth opened to yell.

"Signor di Sala is dead," said Alfredo firmly.

Signor Pozzarelli bit himself short and stared. He obviously hadn't recognized Alfredo till he spoke, and no wonder, a filthy boy in torn peasant clothes, Toni just as bad, and equally unrecognizable, and the dumb servant woman.

"Where . . . ? What . . . ?" he stammered. "The mountain . . ."

"Can we come in? I'll tell you what happened."

"The woman? The idiot?"

"Yes, please. He isn't an idiot. And he was there."

Signor Pozzarelli snorted, shaking his head in bafflement, but let them through and led them into his office. Both windows were smashed in. Glass littered the floor. Without offering any of them a chair he settled himself behind his desk.

"Well?" he snapped, trying to take control of the situation.

Alfredo wasn't put out. He'd thought this all through on his way down the mountain.

"My uncle was a very bad man," he said. "You know that, don't you? But everyone was afraid of him, because he was Master of the Mountain. He was the only one who could control it."

"Peasant gossip," said Signor Pozzarelli.

"You didn't think so when we came here to make my uncle's new will," said Alfredo. "You knew that if he wanted he could have made the mountain burn this whole town to the ground. He pretty well told you that his heir would be able to do that too, didn't he? And it's true. Only I'm not his heir."

Confidently he crossed to the fireplace and lifted the screen away. The fire was laid and ready for lighting. He looked at Toni and nodded.

189

Toni merely glanced toward the hearth and paper, and kindling and logs were instantly ablaze, and flames roaring up the chimney.

"Signor Pozzarelli," said Alfredo formally. "Let me introduce Signor Antonio di Sala, my uncle's only son, his true heir. You knew that, didn't you? He was the person my uncle named in his old will, wasn't he? He is now Master of the Mountain. The mountain destroyed my uncle and chose him instead. He has all my uncle's powers. He put the mountain back to sleep after it had destroyed my uncle. I saw him do it, I was there. Toni isn't a fool, Signor Pozzarelli. You understand? Look at him."

In fact Signor Pozzarelli was already doing so, and now watched Toni hold up a warning finger and simply nod. His smile was only half humorous. Signor Pozzarelli understood.

"You've still got the old will, haven't you?" said Alfredo. "I was right about Signor Antonio being named as heir? And the new one? My uncle had copies, I suppose, but they're gone — the mountain's buried them."

"In that case I have the only copies, Signor Alfredo."

"May I see them, please."

Signor Pozzarelli rose and crunched across the splintered glass to rummage among the pile of folders on the shelves behind him. He handed the two wills across. There was a sheet of paper attached to the old one with a note saying that it had been superseded by a new will dated last Tuesday. At the back of the new one was the list of Uncle Giorgio's properties that Signor Pozzarelli had mentioned that day. Alfredo glanced through it. It looked as if Uncle

Giorgio had owned practically half the town, and a lot of farms, too. The inn had belonged to him, and so had Signor Pozzarelli's own house. He detached the list and put it at the back of the old one.

"Would this still be valid if the other one disappeared?" he said.

"Indeed yes. But . . ."

Alfredo turned and placed the new will and the note that had been with the old one on the burning logs and stood and watched them burn, thinking about his next move.

"I'm sorry," he said, turning back. "You were going to tell me something."

"Er, well, yes. It was that the willful destruction of a valid legal document is a serious criminal offense, but perhaps, since you were the named beneficiary . . ."

"It didn't happen," said Alfredo. "There's two other witnesses here. But there was something else . . . Signor Antonio will be twenty-one next year, won't he? And then he'll be able to turn a tenant out of his house if he wants?"

"Not if he thereby breaks the contract of tenancy," said Signor Pozzarelli anxiously. His own contract had only a couple of years to run, Alfredo had noticed.

"Yes, of course," he said. "But suppose somebody'd been a loyal servant to the di Salas for ages, he could give them their house as a reward."

"Indeed yes, he could."

"I was just interested. I'm sorry. But that's all right then, and you're still Toni's guardian. He'll need somewhere to live, and some money for clothes and so on. I hope you can fix all that."

"I will start to look for a suitable property first thing to-morrow. In the meanwhile you'll stay at the inn, perhaps."

"I'm afraid you'll have to take us across, or they'll throw us out, looking like this. You'll have to tell them something about what's happened. It's a bit difficult. My uncle was a sorcerer, as well as being Master of the Mountain. He could make gold, and he was going to try and live forever. He was going to use me for that. That's why he made me his heir, you see. The same with Toni, long ago. Annetta thought it was because he wanted Toni to become a sorcerer, like him-self, and she thought that was wicked, so she taught him how to pretend to be an idiot. That's right, isn't it Annetta?"

She nodded confidently. Her lips twitched. He turned back to the lawyer.

"Toni didn't dare learn to talk in case my uncle found out, which is why I'm talking for him now. The important thing he wants me to tell everyone is that he doesn't want to be a sorcerer. He wants to be a good Master, and look af-ter everyone, and keep them safe from the mountain. Will you tell people that? They'll listen to you. They all know the mountain's got to have a Master, don't they, though I don't expect they talk about it much."

"Indeed yes, indeed."

Signor Pozzarelli paused and turned to Toni.

"Signor Antonio, I am honored to be the first to wel-come you to your inheritance."

Alfredo smiled to himself. *Barring an Angel or two,* he thought. *And the salamanders.*

EPILOGUE

"*I WILL LIFT UP MINE EYES UNTO THE HILLS, FROM whence cometh my help. . . .*"

The choir was singing with a new gusto. Behind and above them on the right-hand side of the church the two Signori di Sala stood in the ancient stalls of their family and sang with the choir. Such behavior was by any standards eccentric, but the oddities of the di Salas had always been tolerated on the excuse that they were generous patrons of the church. An excuse was needed, of course, since nobody cared to mention the unwisdom of offending the Master of the Mountain. So the antics of the two Signori were watched with more or less benignity (according to how many marriageable daughters the watcher had) by the other gentry, all of them now also occupying the ancient stalls of their families on either side of the church.

Signor Antonio's immense wealth would have excused almost anything, but in spite of his curious upbringing and dubious parentage he was beginning to be well regarded for his own sake. He was a handsome young man who carried himself without any swagger or vanity, and was so strangely assured that despite his still awkward manner of speech—and even that was steadily improving—one rapidly forgot his previous life. Indeed the story of his long pretense at idiocy had a certain romantic allure.

And, in a nutshell, from the very first he had done all the right things. Letting it be known that unlike his uncle he would welcome the return of the gentry to their own stalls was just a minor example. The whole town still spoke of the great party he had given to celebrate his coming of age, held down at the harbor since the new Casa di Sala had not yet begun to be built, with three dance floors and three separate bands, two of them imported from Palermo, and not only a full-scale banquet for the gentry but generous feasting for everyone and colossal fireworks from barges in the harbor to end it all, while the mountain drowsed benignly above.

Memories in such places as this were very long, going back many generations in some families. All Uncle Giorgio's books and records were buried with the rest of his secrets beneath the lava flow that covered Casa di Sala, but once people had decided that it was safe to talk to Alfredo they had told him enough for him to be able to piece together the history of the Mastership for over three hundred years. There had been good Masters and bad, though all had been held in awe for what they were and what they could do. Some had been easygoing and kept open house, some had been remote scholars, some—Uncle Giorgio was not the first—had been seduced by their strange power to acquire even more dangerous powers, which had turned them wicked. These, in the end, the mountain had rejected and destroyed. Almost as disastrously, Alfredo's great-grandfather had been a drunkard, neglecting his duties and reducing his own estate to ruinous poverty. This no doubt was why Uncle Giorgio had set out to repair his fortunes by accomplishing the First Great Work.

No wonder, then, that those who lived at the foot of the mountain looked forward to Toni's Mastership with hope.

Alfredo was aware of all this, but just now was wholly absorbed in the music—not, like Toni, rapt and oblivious in his singing, because his own voice was in the process of breaking and he was singing almost sotto voce, glad of the confident baritone beside him. Instead he was listening critically to the sounds from the choir. It was now four months since he and Toni and Signor Pozzarelli had traveled to Palermo to look for a professional choirmaster. Toni had offered a suitable salary to compensate for the move to a small provincial town, so they'd interviewed several applicants and chosen the youngest, himself a one-time choirboy, now at the start of his career. His effect was already noticeable. The setting of the psalm was ambitious for a country church, but the choir were making a go of it. The new tenor held things together, and both old basses were improving Sunday by Sunday. Best of all, everyone, even the most recalcitrant treble, was beginning to sound interested.

Yes, Alfredo thought, he could live with this. There was no need to break his ties with the mountain, as Father had been forced to do. The new house, when it was built, up among the vineyards, would not be a copy of the old one.

He and Annetta and Toni had discussed it in detail. It would in fact be two houses to start with, one for Annetta and Toni and himself to live in like ordinary people, with Annetta still doing most of the cooking, and a girl, perhaps, to do the cleaning. But that would be screened behind a much grander-seeming main house, with space for a sensible level of entertaining, including, of course, a music room. One day, probably, Toni would marry—though it was no use the two Signorinas Ricardi competing with each other in cuteness and coyness from across the aisle. He would choose a girl who wanted to live the kind of life he liked—the innkeeper's younger daughter seemed a good bet, and Annetta approved of her. But even when a third house had to be built for them the new Casa di Sala would still be smaller than Uncle Giorgio's. And it would feel like somebody's home.

But that wasn't a matter of bricks and tiles and beams and furniture and so on. A home is a place where a few people feel at home with each other, and Toni and Annetta and Alfredo already felt at home in the farmhouse they'd moved into—one of Toni's that happened to be empty. Alfredo didn't think much about his own future beyond the next few years. One day, presumably, he, too, might marry and have children—not just to ensure that the mountain would always have a di Sala to be its Master—but it was still hard for him to imagine it. Rather less vaguely he hoped to travel, and listen to the great choirs of Rome and Venice, and farther afield—there was said to be wonderful music in Vienna, and even in far-off London. But however far he went and for however many years, one thing was certain—he would in the end come back. He had given himself to the mountain, and the mountain had saved him. These fields and vineyards and olive groves, these woods, this single, harsh, barren peak with the undying fire beneath it, this was where he belonged, and nowhere else.

ABOUT THE AUTHOR

PETER DICKINSON is the author of many books for adults and young readers and has won numerous awards, including the Carnegie Medal (twice), the *Guardian* Award and the Whitbread Award (also twice). His novel *Eva* was a *Boston Globe–Horn Book* Fiction Honor Book. *Eva* was also selected as an ALA Best Book for Young Adults, as were his novels *AK* and *A Bone from a Dry Sea*. *The Lion Tamer's Daughter and Other Stories* was chosen as a Best Book of the Year by *School Library Journal*. His most recent book was *The Ropemaker*, which was selected as a Michael L. Printz Honor Book for Young Adults by the American Library Association. Peter Dickinson has four grown children and lives in Hampshire, England, with his wife, the writer Robin McKinley.